BORROWED FROM TOMORROW

Tales Told by an Idiot

VAIBHAV SRIVASTAV

FROG BOOKS

ISBN 978-93-52017-38-6
MRP : 225/-
Copyright © Vaibhav Srivastav, 2016

First published in India 2016 by Frog Books
An imprint of Leadstart Publishing Pvt Ltd
1 Level, Trade Centre
Bandra Kurla Complex
Bandra (East) Mumbai 400 051 India
Telephone: +91-22-40700804
Fax: +91-22-40700800
Email: info@leadstartcorp.com
www.leadstartcorp.com / www.frogbooks.net

Sales Office:
Unit No.25/26, Building No.A/1,
Near Wadala RTO,
Wadala (East), Mumbai – 400037 India
Phone: +91 22 24046887

US Office:
Axis Corp, 7845 E Oakbrook Circle
Madison, WI 53717 USA

Disclaimer: The Views expressed in this book are those of the Author and do not pertain to be held by the Publisher.

Editor: Shilpi Sinha
Cover: Nishant
Layouts: Logiciels Info Solutions Pvt. Ltd.

Typeset in Palatino Linotype
Printed at Repro

For Mummy and Papa

Who Helped Me Swim in a Sea of Stories

Acknowledgements

This book is a labour of love which has taken me many years to write. The stories came to me from my experiences and travels, from meeting people and from this stranger than fiction world that we live in. I would like to thank Leadstart Publishing for helping me transfer my stories from back-of-classroom registers and scattered word documents into a book which you hold in your hand presently.

This book would not have been possible without my parents who told me that reading stories is essential to growing up and my brother who showed me magic where there was none.

This journey in writing was made easier by the constant goading, encouragement, threats and loving messages of Sanju Dada, Nikhil, Adi, Push, Manuj, Sanshit, Sonam, J, Shanks, Mota, Dey, Joshi and Pandey.

About The Author

Born in a small town of UP called Gonda, Vaibhav Srivastav spent his childhood in small cities like Sonpur, Lucknow and Baroda, studied in Banaras and Delhi, and worked in Bangalore and Mumbai. He has devoured a veritable feast of novels and short stories from an early age. During this journey of living in a wide variety of cities and towns he has collected innumerable experiences, and these experiences have helped him put his stories on paper.

Vaibhav presently works as an Area Business Manager of Mumbai for Titan Company Ltd. He has studied management from the Indian Institute of Foreign Trade, Delhi and engineering from Institute of Technology, Banaras Hindu University.

He runs a blog on films called Filmistani (www.philmistani. in) and is also a moderator of a popular socio-political humour page on Facebook called Bhak Sala which is currently followed by more than five and a half lakh people.

The collection deals with tales of magical realism, stories wherein ordinary humans are placed in extraordinary conditions, reflections on mortality, divinity and also certain stories about love, longing and nostalgia.

CONTENTS

THIEF

I can't claim to have personally met all the people whose experiences (or non-experiences) no better call them stories, I have written below. However, I have met and perhaps even known the chief influence behind each one of them (including mine). He calls himself a thief. He says it's the most suitable word to describe him.

From his accounts of what he had stolen from people, I have structured a tale without even talking to all the people involved. I am a writer; I have the liberty to do that.

Anil used to tell his non-smoker friends, 'For the serious smoker the first cigarette in the morning is the most important. Because as the day progresses, after five or six sticks the nicotine stops hitting you. Sure the smoke gets through, and I personally can't do without my daily pack of ten, but I tell you, it's the first one in the morning that I really relish.'

Anil's parents, like unassuming parents of many college going kids, didn't know that their son smoked. They knew that some of his friends did, and his mother attributed the mild smell of burnt tobacco to the company he kept.

Anil practised the mouth freshener and mint routine and used it to camouflage the after-smoke stink. He hadn't been caught till now and did not intend to get caught in future either.

For his early morning smoke he had a simple plan. Smoking anywhere near his home would be dangerous. College started at nine in the morning so he would tell his parents that he was going jogging each morning to a park a couple of kilometres away from the house.

So as not to arouse suspicion he donned the complete jogging gear and drove his bike to the park while buying his daily pack of ten from an all-night cigarette shop en route.

It was a cold and bland December day. Anil followed his daily drill and parked his bike next to the gate. He was mildly disappointed that there was someone else sitting on his regular bench. This guy was wearing a dirty and old blue jacket and had a face that was too vague to remember. He decided to ignore him and his eyes went in search of the tight-sweatshirt-thin-bra girl who jogged at the same park.

He saw her at a distance and leaned back on the bench. He crossed his legs and opened the pack of cigarettes. He lit one and pulled long and hard at it. The first drag of the day. The smoke made its way down his throat and into his lungs.

He waited for the nicotine to hit.

He waited for the high.

And nothing happened.

It felt strange. He looked at the cigarette butt for the brand label. Then he pulled at it again. He inhaled the smoke deeply but still didn't feel a thing. After a few drags he got frustrated and fished out the packet from his pocket to see if they were real or some cheap imitation.

The pack seemed alright, at least by whatever experience that he had. He thought perhaps this was a defective stick.

He quickly lit another one, cursing the manufactures for the defective piece.

Still nothing. His nerves seemed to be numb to the smoke. Had he started smoking so much that even his morning-*sutta* had lost its pleasure? The last cigarette that he had smoked was nearly ten hours ago. There must be some effect!

In his frustration he extinguished the second cigarette too and vowed not to smoke again. At least for a while.

The man sitting next to him rose and walked a few paces away. Then he turned to face him. He blew smoke towards Anil.

The man hadn't been smoking.

Anil was dumbstruck; before he could even think of reacting, the man had already disappeared behind the wall and exited the park.

Karan was in an office with a six-day week. The work hours too were long and hard. Every employee was expected to put in at least twelve hours each day, and with words like 'Global-meltdown' and 'Recession' floating in the air, no one dared to slack. The load was strenuous, but the remuneration for the pain was good. He earned upwards of a lakh rupees per month and was steadily rising up the corporate ladder.

Sadly he had no time to spend the money he was earning. He had a plush house, and he could easily afford it with his income. But it was an hour's drive from his office. Twelve hours at the workplace and two hours of commute left him with only less than ten hours at home.

He'd been married for two years and all he could be with his wife was for three to four hours each day apart from sleeping, and with all the fatigue from work he brought home, most of what they did at night was just sleep together.

Over the months he could see his wife's visible frustration. There was dryness in her voice and she mostly seemed aloof.

Moments of romance did come by, some rainy nights, an old favourite movie, when he got something nice for her as a small gift, but mostly their marriage seemed to be going downhill.

He then decided to make the best of Sundays. Although his main focus was his work he really liked his wife and wanted to make her feel better.

Each Sunday he woke up late with his wife and made breakfast for her as she woke up. They at times behaved as teenagers in the corner seats of some obscure movie theatre in the evenings. And for dinner he reserved a table at some posh restaurant and she really did feel happy. On Sundays his wife was a different woman. Or perhaps he was a different man.

Like any given Sunday, that day too the couple entered a swank restaurant, feeling happy and content. And because they frequented it once or twice a month, the maître d' knew them quite well and always gave them a good table. Karan had a reputation as a generous tipper, so the service was smooth too.

'What would you like my love?' He asked her after they had settled down.

'Oh for starters the usual, and for main course, surprise me'. She trilled happily.

'Surprise you? Ok...interesting'.

He ordered his favourite dishes from the menu. Apart from the fact that it was a special evening with his wife, the food was always nice.

A whole week of horrible lunch at the office cafeteria and dinner prepared by a mostly miffed wife, his taste buds could always use the treat. He always waited for Sunday evenings for a chance to eat something nice.

After placing the order he moved closer to his wife. In the candle light they whispered sweet nothings to each other and held hands. After some time he saw a man from a table nearby staring at them. He had long hair and was wearing a brown kurta. He was the only one who seemed out of place in the crowd at the restaurant.

He decided to ignore the man. His wife was very pretty and he was used to people staring at her. In fact it gave him a glow of pride, that others were envious of him.

The starters arrived. The couple fed the portions to each other with the forks. However today the food didn't taste good to Karan. In fact it tasted of nothing at all.

'How's the food, jaan?' He asked his wife.

'Mmmm...it's good ... especially because I am eating it from your hand'. She said 'And how do you like it?'

Not to sound unromantic, Karan lied, 'When my love's feeding me how can the food be bad.'

He did not mention that the food was tasteless. Perhaps his wife had some extra sensitive taste buds, or maybe his had died from all the bad food at the office cafeteria. The food at the restaurant was always excellent, and his wife seemed to find it alright, he decided to give it the benefit of doubt.

He somehow finished the dish and waited for the main course. The food was ash in his mouth. He again asked his wife, 'Jaan, is the taste okay?'

'Yeah... but I think it is a bit bland than the usual'.

'You think so too, na? The taste is not the same. I think we should call the chef.'

'Oh come on jaan, it's just a bit off colour. Why call the chef for that? We are regular customers here ...'

'Yeah, that's the whole point. We are regular customers. The food should be good for us.'

'Oh kay...maybe we can tell one of the waiters to take the dish back and rework it a bit.'

Karan's growing anger subsided. This seemed like a decent solution. He called the waiter and handed him the dish. Since the waiters knew Karan by face, he didn't haggle over his complain and took the dish back to the kitchen.

After some time the chef sent the food back to the table, spicing it up a bit. He too didn't mind this one time criticism by a regular customer.

Unfortunately for Karan, the food was still the same. His wife considered it to be alright. The man sitting on the next table gulped down a whole glass of water in one go. Karan became very angry.

He called the waiter.

'Is this what you call an improvement?'

'Sir?'

'I told you to go fix it, not just heat it and bring it back.'

'I think the chef did his best sir, and this is the food we serve all our customers. We addressed your complaint too. We normally don't do that.'

'But I can't stand the food today! What have you people done to it?' Karan was almost shouting by now.

His wife said, 'Jaanu please calm down.'

The waiter too said quietly, 'Sir, please don't make a scene here. You are disturbing the other customers.'

'Call your manager!'

'I'll do that sir. Please do not raise your voice.'

The waiter went to fetch the manager.

'Honey, what's wrong? Why are you getting so worked up?' The wife said, 'The food tastes fine now. In fact it is spicier than I'd like it to be.'

'Dear ...' Karan seemed helpless now.

'Yes jaanu, what is it?'

'I can't taste a thing!'

'What?'

'Yes dear… nothing! Can't taste anything at all.'

'Even this spicy food?'

'Honey…this spicy food tastes not just bland but completely tasteless.'

'Oh… come on sweetheart. I think we should get you to a doctor. I think there's something wrong with your tongue.'

The manager walked up to their table and asked 'Is there a problem sir?'

Karan didn't answer anything. His wife said in a soft voice, 'Yes there is a problem. My husband's not feeling well. Please bring us the bill, we are leaving.'

Karan paid the bill and left. He decided he was going to the doctor to test his tongue the next morning. He dreaded the fact that he wouldn't be able to taste food again.

The waiter went to the man sitting on the table next to him and said, 'Sir, will a salad be all?'

Simran and Ankit didn't like frequenting lover's spots, or at least popular lover's spots. They found it hard to attain intimacy in the throng of other couples present around them for the same reason.

They had been lovers for over a year. They were in the same college and their affair was common knowledge all over. Even then they didn't like to be in the public eye. They took risks and frequented desolate locations where they could be almost alone.

One such place was 'Kaladevi Fort', a derelict outpost of an old princely state from the British Raj times. It was a ruin of a fort which couldn't have been much in its prime either. Yet there were small enclosures and shades which could provide enough privacy for lovers. Apart from Simran and Ankit, other couples too used the place, but they were too few in number to bother them. And on most days the place was empty.

Simran really loved Ankit, and whenever he seemed to be in a mood she brought him to Kaladevi Fort.

That day too they had some minor argument and Simran felt sorry for it. She wanted to make him feel better, and suggested a trip to Kaladevi. Ankit wasn't in the mood. He still felt slightly angry and didn't want to take a romantic trip.

'I don't wanna go there today.' He said.

'Please dear, I said na I am sorry. Come let's go there. You will feel better,' then she whispered, 'I will make you feel better.'

After some time Ankit relented, he figured out that the trip could do something in the way of making his mood better. Besides, going to Kaladevi was always fun.

The fort was located on a small hill, in the day it was a good place for lovers and in the evening it was taken over by smokers and dopers. Ankit and Simran parked their bike near their favourite spot and went to sit comfortably in the shade of a torn down wall. Some thirty feet away a man sat on the edge of the hill. He was wearing a black Jim Morrison tee shirt and jeans. He was smoking cigarettes and generally minding his own business. So Simran and Ankit weren't particularly bothered. Besides, he had his back to them.

Simran looked at Ankit and could see the slightly sad expression on his face. She smiled when she thought that he looked kind of cute with a frown and drooping eyes. She kissed him on the cheek and waited for him to respond.

All he did was put his arm across her shoulder and pull her closer towards him.

She sighed and nestled against him, drumming her fingers on his chest and waiting for his mood to get better on its own. She tried to slip her hand inside his shirt but he stopped her. He didn't jerk her hand away; rather he held it a little too firmly for her comfort.

'*Jaan*, you are hurting me!'

He released her hand and said, 'Sorry.'

She pulled herself even closer and turned his face towards her. '*Jaanu* ...' she cooed, 'I love you."

He replied sullenly, 'Me too ...'

'Your mood is still not good, please *Jaan*! Don't be like this. I love you, you know na how much I love you.'

He mumbled under his breath, 'Yeah, maybe.'

She sat up straight and said, '*Jaanu* please, improve your mood! I am so sorry about yesterday. I said na, I won't repeat it again. Please accept my sorry, I love you!'

Ankit turned his face slightly away and said, 'Love you too.'

'Come on my love, there is something that is still bothering you. Tell me, tell me what it is that you are thinking about.'

Ankit closed his eyes and took a deep breath. He opened his mouth to say something but didn't. Simran cupped his face in her hands and coaxed him to answer again. 'Tell me *Jaan*, what is it.' She leaned close to kiss his forehead and whispered, 'You are my life.'

He opened his eyes and glared at her, 'You know what, I don't think that you do.'

She leant back, 'What!'

He repeated himself, 'I don't think you love me.'

And in that moment Simran was scared. She was afraid that Ankit would leave her. She loved him with all her life and couldn't even bear the thought of living without him.

'*Jaanu*, please don't say that. I love you, I love you so much.'

'I don't know.' He said, 'But right now I don't think that you love me.'

She was crestfallen; the past year seemed to account for nothing right now. All the loving she had for him, did it not account for anything?

'Why do you feel so?' She asked him, her voice was quavering, and there were tears forming at the corner of her eyes.

'I don't know, I just can't feel that you love me right now.'

"Please Jaanu, don't even think of such a thing. You don't even know how much I love you.'

'Okay, then tell me how much you love me. Cause I don't even know, isn't it?' Ankit said coldly.

Simran felt helpless. She wanted to bang her head on the wall, and felt like slapping herself. She was crying already, Ankit closed his eyes so that he didn't have to see her in such a miserable condition.

Simran wanted to prove to Ankit how much she loved him, she wanted to list out all the things that she had done for him, all the pains she had taken, the lies to her parents, the friends she had ignored, everything she could recall. However, she couldn't bring herself to do that. Shouldn't Ankit realize this on his own? Why should she have to tell him?

Ankit opened his eyes and looked at her. Simran couldn't even be angry at the sad little face. Perhaps there was something less in the way she loved him. She resolved to love him even more.

'Ankit dear...'

'Yeah?'

'You know na...I can't live without you.'

Ankit started looking down and said drily, 'Don't give me fake promises.'

She didn't know what to say. She did not know what to do. All she knew was that she loved the boy sitting in front of her and currently it seemed that their relationship hung by a thin string. She wished for some magic, anything to make this moment alright.

She leant over him and said, 'Please hug me.'

They hugged for a while and Simran cried silently on his shoulder, not able to think of anything. She started kissing him on his neck and on his cheeks. She turned his face and kissed him on his lips, first gently and then parting his lips with her tongue she gave him a warm and deep tongue kiss, tasting her own tears.

He held her close with one hand in her hair and the other at her lower back. They shared a long kiss, and Simran felt the warmth flow through her body. When they broke for breath, she looked at him with limitless adoration in her eyes. Resting her head on his chest she asked him, '*Jaanu* how did it feel?'

He said, 'Nothing.'

Simran wasn't sure she heard him right. She asked him again, her voice shaking. Ankit repeated his answer and said, 'I felt nothing in your kiss. No love, no hunger, no desire. And I am being honest with you Simran, it didn't make me feel good. I think you kissed me because of some misplaced sense of sympathy that you have for me.'

Simran started getting a serious headache. This frustration seemed to be harming her. She wanted to do something bad to herself; she wanted to bleed, to shout, what had she done to deserve this? She was angry now, 'I want to go home,' she said between sobs.

Ankit saw her and realized that he felt sorry for her. He didn't want to hurt her this way. He said, 'Come on, let's stay for a while.'

'No! I want to go home. Drop me there or I will go on my own.'

Ankit said, 'Sorry...'

'Sorry! What sorry? I hate you!' She began banging her fists on his chest, 'I hate you! I hate you so much! Don't talk to me.'

Ankit hugged her again. He waited for her to calm down. He was stroking her hair as she mumbled angrily in his ear.

He saw the man in black-shirt and blue jeans throw a cigarette butt down the hill and get up and walk away. Perhaps that man didn't want to hear the rest of the argument, he had already overheard a lot.

Shivam Gupta sat on the edge of the bed of a cheap hotel room where lodging was charged on an hourly basis. It was one of those seedy joints that openly had a bad reputation.

There was no check-in time or check-out time. Any room could be taken for as long or as little time as required. The hotel management did not mind because they knew the purpose of the customers coming there. They did not ask for any ID or paper work, only ready cash paid upfront.

The half-naked girl lying on the bed was a friend's girlfriend. The friend had left the city for a year and he had willingly stepped into his shoes to take care of her.

He flirted with her shamelessly, took her out to nice places, long drives and generally made her feel good whenever she missed her boyfriend.

Of course he did all this with the intention of getting her into bed someday.

It took him a long time to do it, but he pursued her with zeal. Her initial rebuttals had made it an ego thing for him. He seduced her slowly, breaking the shell around her, taking down her defences. And he knew that being away from her boyfriend for such a long time there was a certain need that wasn't getting fulfilled.

He started by kissing her at the right moments, stealing kisses, holding her hand whenever they got close. She held back initially, and he got away with everything by acting like the cute naughty boy. Then slowly she relented, letting him kiss whenever he wanted to. She started enjoying his touch, at times pretending to herself that it was her boyfriend and not him.

She never fell in love with him, still all his sweet talk somehow convinced her that what she was doing was right. And because she felt guilty, she loved her boyfriend all the more. Never ever letting the poor boy get even a whiff of what was happening.

And then on one of their dates he said quite bluntly, 'I want to sleep with you.'

She was shocked. They had been making out for quite some time now and she really liked it, but she wasn't going to have sex with him. It would be way too much. In fact what they were doing already was way too much.

'No!' She half shouted.

'Why not? Don't you like what we do?' He said with a cruel smile playing upon his face.

'Oh shut up!' She said, and ran away from the restaurant.

She went home and thought about her boyfriend. What would happen to him if he got to know? She loved him and didn't want to break his heart.

And then she thought of Shivam, and she hated herself for all that they did together. The worst part was that she couldn't shut out graphic images of the two of them having sex.

That night after talking to her boyfriend she called him up.

'I knew you would call,' he said.

That bastard, that condescending bastard. She wanted to shout at him, call him names and abuse him in general, but instead she said, 'What if he gets to know?'

He said, 'Don't worry. He will never get to know. Do you think that I would tell him...that I had sex with his girlfriend?'

She knew that at this moment he would have that evil grin on his face. She couldn't think why she wanted him. But she knew she did.

'You don't have to say that out loud you know.' She was feeling angry, more so with herself than the creep that she was talking to on the phone.

And yet she knew that she was ready.

'When...' She asked him.

'When what?' He teased her.

She took a deep breath and said, 'You know what I am talking about.'

After a small pause he said, 'Tomorrow at four I'll pick you up from your office.' And then he hung up on her.

The next day he booked a room for three hours in advance at that obscure hotel. He paid the hundred rupee per hour rate and then went to pick her up.

She looked all decked up in makeup and everything, and had dressed better than what she used to dress usually. He imagined what she would look without her dress and couldn't wait to take it off her.

He felt her hand shaking as he led her to the room. He closed the door and started kissing her. She shut her eyes and let her body go limp. She wanted to concentrate only on the feeling and nothing else. Shivam's body was an object, just something to satisfy herself.

Shivam was enjoying himself. He saw this as a fulfilment of a fantasy. And he wanted the pleasure to be as prolonged as possible.

He took off her clothes and pushed her against the bed. He used all his practiced moves and was glad to see her body responding. He kissed her, bit her, stroked her until she came to a frenzied state of excitement and said, 'Do what you want with me...please.'

Shivam removed his own clothes and started kissing her again.

At that point something drained out of him.

He lost all sensation of the pleasure that he should be feeling. He still had an erection but sex didn't seem to be having any effect. The girl beneath him writhed and moaned in contentment, and yet he felt nothing.

Still he didn't stop. He took this as a test of his masculinity. And after a while the girl shrieked as she climaxed and Shivam still felt nothing.

She went to sleep soon and Shivam set on the edge of the bed, feeling frustrated, impotent and unsatisfied. Then it struck him that perhaps instead of his virility, there was some problem with the girl.

'Cheap, frigid whore.' He thought, and angrily put on his clothes. He then woke up the girl to shout and vent his frustration.

Outside at the reception counter the two clerks discussed the customer who had just checked out.

'This guy always come alone, and stays for an hour and leaves. I wonder why.'

'Perhaps he jerks off listening to all the sex. Bloody pathetic loner.' They both laughed and then paid no further heed to the loner.

I was sitting at my favourite tea and cigarette stall with my friend Krishna. We were both billowing Gold Flake smoke and sipping special *chai* when I told him, 'I broke up with Anjali an hour ago.'

Krishna spurted out the tea that was in his mouth and said, 'What!'

'Calm down...calm down.' I told him, 'it was meant to happen. We had been arguing so much lately, it was hard to live with each other.'

'But...when?'

'Told you...an hour ago, on the phone. I was sitting here waiting for you and I called her up. I wanted to give our relationship another chance, yet again.'

Krishna waited for me to speak further.

I took a long drag from my cigarette and played with the thick stream of smoke. I was enjoying the look of puzzlement on his face; he grew impatient and said, 'Well aren't you going to say anything?'

I laughed and said, 'What is there to say. I got a waiting signal; most probably she was talking to that bastard. I don't know why but I was beyond care, I disconnected the phone and waited for her to call back. I knew she would, and she did.'

I was enjoying the impatience on Krishna's face; he had had a long time crush on Anjali and really looked forward to hearing any bit of gossip about my ex-girlfriend. He said, 'And then? What did she say...what happened?'

'She asked me what I wanted, and I told her that I loved her just to frustrate her. She got irritated and said that she was going to cut the phone unless I had something important to say. I repeated myself and said I LOVE YOU. She started shouting, calling me names and abusing me in general.'

'What exactly did she say?'

'Her usual statement, that I did not love her and that I had never loved her. It makes me angry to hear her talk like this. But I was in the mood for some emotional terrorism. I replied to her sweetly, telling her all the things that I had ever done for her.' I paused for a while, inhaling the smoke and reflecting on my love life, 'I don't know. Maybe she was right, maybe I never really loved her as much as I should have, or could have.'

Krishna was on the edge of the bench by now, 'Are you sure it is a break up? Could be a lover's tiff, I mean you guys have always had a violent love story.'

I smiled and said, 'Wait till you hear the rest of it. When she had finished with the name calling and everything she paused for breath. Then I started to speak. I called her a few names myself, giving an outlet to my pent up anger. And I didn't stop.'

'Well! What did you say?'

I drummed my fingers on the wooden bench and said, 'Tirikit-dha, tirikit-dha, tirikit-dha.'

'What does that mean?'

'It means that I said all the things that I had never said to her. I wanted to hurt her, to make her heart bleed, to make her cry. I wanted to do all the bad things that I could do to her, for everything that she had done to me.'

Krishna sighed, 'That's bad. How could you be so cruel?'

I said, 'Because I knew that it was the last time that I was talking to her. I don't want to talk to her ever again. I used to love her, but I don't know, all the feelings are in a weird state right now...almost ephemeral....'

'And...?'

'And she started crying. She said that she couldn't live like this anymore. Well neither could I. I told her that I thought I had lost her, but in reality she was never really ever there. And then we took pleasure in berating each other. I think this was the most interesting conversation that I ever had with her.'

'You bastard...' Krishna said, 'You are smiling! You should be singing some filmy breakup song right now, and instead you actually seem happy!'

'Ha ha...' I said, 'And then she said "I want a break up. I want a break up now!" I too said, "Go to hell my lovely. A big wet kiss to you." And then I ended the call, and have screened her number.'

Krishna threw his cigarette in the dust bin and said, 'So is that it? Over?'

'Yeah. I think this is final, this is goodbye etc.' and then I actually started singing a song about good bye by one of my favourite rock bands.

Krishna patted my shoulder to show his sympathy, he asked me, 'How do you feel?'

'To tell you the truth, I feel cheated.'

'Cheated...why?'

'I don't know, may be because I don't feel anything. I don't feel that it has been good riddance, I don't feel bad about the fact that I just broke up. In fact, to put it simply I don't feel anything at all about what happened just now.'

'So how do you feel cheated then?'

'I feel that I have been cheated out of my pain, all my emotions. I want to feel something, I would give anything in this world to feel something about my break up. I mean, I did love her! And no matter whatever she said, I never stopped loving her while we were still together. How can heartbreak be so painless? I feel like I am under the effect of some emotional anaesthesia.'

Krishna was perplexed. 'What! You are sad because you are not feeling sad?'

'Ha ha…isn't it ironic? But I am not sad, I am frustrated rather. Come on! I deserve to feel!' And then I looked up at the heavens hoping for some bolt of emotional lightening to strike me and fill up the emptiness that I was feeling (or not feeling).

I lit another cigarette as I tried to read Krishna's face; I wanted to know what was going on in his mind right now. Was he happy that I had broken up with Anjali? Or the fact that she was single again, and hence more 'available' than she used to be. And I could see that he was trying hard to suppress a smirk.

His question was one that I had expected, 'So what happens between Anjali and you now?'

'Nothing, she is out of my life. And I am out of hers. We didn't even exchange letters or any major gifts, so there is nothing to give back or take.'

Krishna waited for a while; he didn't want to be tactless. Still he asked me, 'Are you sure this is the final goodbye? I mean you guys are not going to get back together, are you?'

I laughed at him, 'You are really hopeful, aren't you?'

He fumbled, 'About what? Look, I didn't mean anything okay? I mean, I am sad for you. And in a way happy too, because this relationship was hurting you so much. Perhaps life would now be better for both of you, isn't it?'

'I don't know whether life would be better or worse, and presently I don't think that I care. We smoked in silence as I searched hard for sadness inside me. My love life was over, and my break up was violent, yet I felt very *Zen* about it. And the worst part was that I really didn't know why. And because of this rather sedated state of mind I didn't even know whether I wanted to know about it or not.

In all this confusion I didn't notice the man who had come to sit next to me. He borrowed a matchstick and lit his own cigarette.

Krishna opened his mouth to say something but it was that man sitting on my left who spoke, 'Tell me, how you feel?'

I was perplexed at this query from a perfect stranger, I asked him, 'And what is that to you sir?'

He said, 'How you feel has a lot to do with me. In fact it has everything to do with me.'

Krishna and I looked at him with wonder, who was this guy? Some sort of con man? Should the two of us stand up and leave?

I asked him, 'Who are you?'

He smiled and said, 'I am a thief.'

Well that's saying a lot. I mean, I hadn't seen any thief admitting his occupation in my entire life, not that I had seen or met many thieves.

'What do you mean that you are a thief? And how are you so comfortably sitting there and telling us that you are a thief?'

'I don't mind telling people....especially now...'

'What are you? Some sort of honest thief?'

He said 'I am a thief. And not a very common one.'

'Why, what makes you different? Are you like Robin Hood?' Krishna asked him. The guy laughed and said, 'No I don't think so, I am not like any thief that you have ever come across, be it in real life or in fiction.'

We waited for him to expand upon this statement as he sat there silently smoking his cigarette. He calmly said, 'I steal feelings, and emotions, and sensations.'

It took us some time to digest this, but we still didn't understand him fully. 'Meaning? How do you steal feelings?'

'Well to tell you the truth I am not really sure about the how part. It has been an inherent gift of some sort. Like right now, I stole your feeling of heartbreak.'

Surely a con man, he must have heard the conversation that I was just having with Krishna, and because neither of us had taken the care of being discreet or kept our voices low. Anyone sitting in a five-meter radius could tell that I didn't have the feeling of heartbreak that I was supposed to be having. I did not believe the thief.

He continued, 'See I was sitting right behind you all the time when you were having that conversation with your girl. And it was pretty obvious where that was heading, so I decided that I am going to spare you the pain of the break up by stealing your feelings.'

I was irritated, 'Look mister, whoever you are, *Charandas Chor* or whatever. Please don't make fun of me. As it is I am not going through a very happy phase of my life, I don't want some random guy coming to me and screwing up my mind.'

He said, 'I am not here to screw your mind. I wanted to help you. Tell me, how do you feel? It is important for me to know that.'

I decided to carry on the farce with him and told him how I felt. 'Look whatever it is, I don't feel good. I know I am not feeling bad, but I am not feeling good either. I am not feeling anywhere close to how I want to feel right now.'

The thief was puzzled, he asked me, 'So how exactly do you want to feel right now?'

'I WANT TO FEEL MY HEARTBREAK.' I almost shouted.

He smiled again, 'No need to get so worked up about it. Don't worry; I will give you your feelings back. But why do you want to feel it? Do you not think you are better off without feeling the pain? Isn't it better to be comfortably numb?'

I was angry, but I kept my cool and answered him, 'I want to feel because without it my erstwhile love life would have no significance. I mean, it is important for me. That phase of my life which just ended had a meaning, a part to play. And without this, it wouldn't account to anything at all.'

He thought for a while and said, 'Yeah that's true. I am sorry, I was just trying to help you. I think I will give your feelings back.'

Krishna, who had been quiet for some time suddenly said, 'Do you even believe this guy? What is this shit that he is talking about? Hey mister, are you a magician or something? And give us some proof, thief *sa'ab*, why should we believe that you are telling the truth?'

The thief's face was emotionless, 'I am giving him his feelings back, I think that should be proof enough for what I have just told you.'

We waited in silence for him to mumble some *mantra* or some other mumbo jumbo to prove his point, but he didn't say anything. He didn't even keep on looking at me, to hypnotize me or something.

And then it happened.

A pain rushed through my veins and instantly hit me in the head. I became sad and depressed, and after sitting like that for a while the first word that came to my mind was, 'Anjali.'

And then I started sobbing, there were picture postcards in my brain pointing out to significant events from my love life. 'Anjali…I love her.'

Krishna chipped in, 'Used to love her. You just now said that you don't love her anymore.'

I glared at him and said, 'Yeah…but emotions don't die in a moment. I still have feelings for her.'

'That too you said, there were no feelings anymore. Dude, what's happening to you?'

I said, 'I don't know, I think I am drowning in some emotional flood. A minute ago I wasn't feeling anything for her, or anything because of the break up. But God damn, I miss her so much right now.'

I could easily see the disappointment on Krishna's face. He didn't want me to feel anything at all for her. He asked me again, 'Are you sure?'

'Yeah…I don't know what is happening to me. I was so frustrated a little while ago because I didn't feel anything, and now…now this pain seems to be unbearable.'

The thief coughed slightly, drawing attention to him. The look on his face said 'I-told-you-so.'

We looked at him in amazement as he sat there smoking Wills Classic and being nonchalant. I tried to push thoughts about Anjali from my mind, and I also tried to tell myself that what I was experiencing was something natural and not something that this thief had a hand (or mind) in.

I asked him, 'Er…are you responsible for this?'

'Responsible for what? The pain that you are feeling? I think that's partly because of yourself and also because of what the girl did to you. Now tell me, was the pain worth it.'

Krishna said, 'You mean to say….that you really did steal his emotions, and when you wanted to you gave it back.'

'What can I say? He was the one who wanted to feel his heartbreak, all I did was steal it from him and then later give it back. That is why he felt almost nothing a while ago and presently is so hysterical.'

I still didn't believe him, 'Can you really do that?'

'My friend, I did it for you. I thought maybe I was doing a good deed. But I guess not. Tell me, why do you want to feel your break up? Aren't you better off not feeling the pain?'

In the span of an hour I had felt the extremes of two emotions, one of an almost complete numbness, and the second that of being in hell because my heart was broken by the girl I love. And I really could decide which feeling was better. I told him, 'I think it was better for me to feel the pain, and I told you why, because it adds value to whatever love-life that I had.'

He looked at me and asked, 'Is that the only reason?'

I pondered over it and said, 'No, maybe not. See I am a writer. (He smiled when he heard this.) And how can I write about something that I do not feel anything for. It is important for me to feel the pain.'

We sat in silence for a while, not knowing what to say. We suddenly realized that we had experienced something decidedly supernatural. After sometime I was the first one to speak,

'Seriously, who are you? And how do you do what you claim to?'

'I told you, I am a thief. And I said before, I am not sure myself of the how part.'

'You do magic?'

'Perhaps, yes better to call it magic than to have to explain it. Because I tell you frankly, I don't know how it happens. I can tell you what happens.'

Part of me wanted to believe this thief because of what had happened just now, and it was this part that wanted to ask questions, 'Is it something like hypnotism?'

'I don't know, I just have to be near someone and wish hard to steal their sensations, and then it happens. I was sitting here listening to your phone call, I have seen many heartbroken lovers go to depths in their pain, for once I wanted to save a soul from burning. That is why I tried to save you.'

Krishna's eyes lit up, 'So you are like a Superhero! You go around trying to save people by taking away their pain, right?'

The man's expression turned slightly glum, he said, 'I am not a Superhero, I am a Super thief. I use this gift, or this power to take from other people. And there is nothing that I return to them except frustration and an unsatisfied desire. I tried to help your friend here, and the result was the same.'

I asked him, 'But then why do you do it?'

He laughed again, a dry sarcastic laugh, 'Why? Well that's an easy question to answer, tell me have you ever felt the ultimate high without even actually smoking or drinking? Or how it feels to eat the best food at the best restaurants in the city, when your taste buds are really looking forward for a treat. Or how does it feel to be loved by a very beautiful girl, or to be kissed by her.

I know the joys of an illicit relationship without hurting someone, I feed on their feelings. To me this world is a market, and all the feelings are for me to take. I fed myself till I was satiated and bloated, and I think I grew bored, or hungry for something else.

And then one day I saw a beggar, thin and frail, he was covered with wounds and was perhaps only a few days away from death. I looked at him, and I looked at his miserable life and everything fell into perception. I hated myself in that moment; here I was feeding myself on the happiness and gluttony of others, when all along I could have helped someone.

I decided to take a risk, and I stole his sensations, his pains. I gave him as you yourself put it an *Emotional Anaesthesia*. I saw that his crying had stopped, while my own body was overcome with pain, it was unbearable and I collapsed. But I think it was worth it.

From that day I decided to use my powers to help people, and you my friend were the second such person. However, after seeing what happened with you I will have to be careful in choosing the people I save. I am sorry, I shouldn't have stolen your feelings.'

The three of us sat in silence, Krishna and I trying to digest what we had just heard. Even if this man was lying, this was an incredible tale, and I wanted to hear more of it.

I said, 'Well, there is one way in which you can repay me for what you did.'

'What? I will try, whatever it is.'

'Tell me your story, all of it, all your experiences.'

The thief smiled and said, 'Ha ha, but I don't want to be caught, I have caused pain to many people.'

'Come on, even if people read my story, there would be few who would believe it. Even the people with whom it has happened won't believe it. It is my, Ashish Prakash's promise that you shall be safe. And I don't even know your name just as it is.'

'And that you will never know.' He took a long pause, and said, 'Fine, let's begin, where do you want me to start?'

He proceeded to tell me his story, parts of which I converted to my own tale which you have finished reading just now.

POST MORTEM

As they lowered my casket into the ground and my brother poured the first grains of the ceremonial mud on the wooden board above me, I tried to shout and tell them that I am not dead, I am still conscious. I heard them cry silently, I heard my *Abba* being restrained by his brothers-in-law, and then I heard very little as the coffin was covered by a thick layer of mud. Soon there was complete silence as everyone who had come to my *Janaza* left.

I shouted to call out to all the others lying around me, hoping that there were others who faced the same predicament as I did. Of being dead, but not quite. But my own family couldn't hear me while I shouted from my coffin after regaining consciousness. I didn't even know whether there was a difference between my thought and speech, whether there were actually any words or was it all in my head.

'Anybody there? 'I shouted, 'Can anyone hear me?'

Despite my condition I felt foolish and full of laughter. I was calling out to the dead in a *Qabristan*. I laughed, not knowing how, but fully knowing that my facial features aren't changing. I wanted to sing loudly, to go mad posthumously, and alternately I wanted to cry and laugh out loud.

'I am dead!' I shouted over and over again until I had to stop myself because I heard another voice. I strained myself to hear the source; I could make out the words.

'Don't shout! I am dead but not deaf.'

It was a girl's voice, it was slightly shrill and sounded irritated. I tried to make out the distance between my grave and hers, while I thought of continuing talking with her. I desperately needed to converse.

'Hullo! This is Fahad, I am new here.'

'Don't be absurd, we are all dead, there is no one new here.' The voice replied.

I waited for a while before asking, 'I am sorry, am I disturbing you?'

The voice said, 'Of course you are! I was sleeping!'

I felt intrigued, could we; the 'Not-quite-dead' do that? And what all could we do? I had too many questions that I wanted to ask to this girl. I mentioned this to her. She said, '*Hai Allah!* Can't you let me rest in peace?'

I fell silent, cursing my over-enthusiasm. After a while, I said, 'I am sorry.'

'No, you are not.'

'How can you say that?

'Because you are still not letting me sleep!'

I decided to not disturb her for a while, and stare at the utter darkness in front of me. When I was young, my *Abba* used to tell me stories of people whose *Rooh* left their bodies after death. They were the unfortunates or the criminals who were banished to roam the earth, and couldn't go to either *Dojakh* or *Jannat*. In a way I was sad that my *rooh* hadn't left my body, it would have been better to be able to see the world around me. I tried to light up the dark staring at me by using my imagination.

Unfortunately all I could think of was my accident, of how the car swerved deliberately towards me, all I heard was a loud noise and a sharp pain in my legs. The scene played over and over again in my head until I forced myself to start counting numbers instead. I counted till thirty-six hundred, waiting for an hour to pass. Then I disturbed the lady lying near me again.

'Miss?' I said, trying not to shout, after a while I heard a drowsy reply asking me what I wanted.

'Miss, how are you able to sleep?'

She was slow in her reply, 'It's not that hard, you will get the hang of it in a while, there's not much to do here.'

'I'm sorry, if I'm irritating you, but...isn't it easier to pass the time by talking?'

She took a lot of pauses while replying, and she talked very slowly, sounding tired and weary. 'I don't know. But okay, I can try...'

'I have a lot of questions to ask.'

'And I am not sure whether I have the answers.'

I mentally made a check list of things that I wanted to ask her, and started with the most obvious, 'How are we able to talk?'

She said, 'I didn't know that we could do that until you came around. I knew I was conscious, I knew that I could think, but I didn't know I could speak and be heard until you came and created the ruckus.'

My rationale was that there was a difference between 'Speaking' and 'Thinking', otherwise she would have heard the one hour that I had spent thinking to myself. I asked her, 'How long have you been here?'

'This is one question that I really can't answer, because it is hard to tell. But I guess you can help me on this, you came here a while ago, I died on the fifth of March in 2011, when did you die?'

I knew for sure that I had lost consciousness on the fifteenth of July, on the way to a job interview, dressed in the best of clothes that I had. I didn't tell her anything about how I died, except for the date.

'And the year?' She asked eagerly.

For some reason she was disappointed when I told her that it was 2011. 'I thought at least a year had passed,' she said. I felt sad for her, I asked her what she did to measure time, and she told me that she had continuously counted 604800 seconds to pass a week, but had gone despondent and stopped caring about time all together.

'I pray a lot, all I need is a release from this state. I cannot wait till *Qayamat* to get away from here.

The prospect of what she said scared me. I reasoned that she hadn't spent a long time here, only three months, thus there was every chance that both of us would get freedom from this state, or might learn how to sleep infinitely. If I can't move or see, I wouldn't mind sleeping till *Qayamat* comes. I told her my plans, and sensed a glimmer of hope in her voice.

'I think you are right Mr…what's your name?'

'I…er…I told you my name. I am Fahad.'

I asked her what her name was, she said that she is not the type of girl who would go around telling her name to strangers, after which I distinctively heard muted laughter.

'I beg your pardon miss, my only intention is to talk, and to help us both pass the time that we have to spend here.'

'What can we talk about? I don't even know you!'

'That's the whole point, we have our whole past to talk about. I have twenty-three years of tales to tell you, miss. How old are you?'

This time she laughed loudly and said, 'You are an insolent young man. First you ask an unknown girl what her name is, and then you have the audacity to ask for her age! Have you no manners?'

I was finally getting through to her, the fact that she was laughing made me feel good. 'Miss, don't tell me your name, don't tell me your age, but maybe you can tell me whether you are younger or older than me.'

'I am not telling you anything, you are the one who claims to have twenty three years of tales to tell me. Start doing that, and maybe I will tell you something about me.'

I took my time before replying, talking to me right now was a girl whom I had never seen and would obviously never be able to. I could imagine her to look like any girl I wanted. She could be that girl who used to stop with her friends at the tea-shop near my house and used to wear a different coloured *duppatta* every day. She could be that extremely beautiful girl I shared a rickshaw with once, she would be anyone who I wanted her to be.

And I, Mohd. Fahad, a mediocre student of Lucknow University, I could be a rockstar. I could be Amitabh Bachchan, I could weave an interesting and exciting life story, totally different from how I had spent my life till now.

'Please allow me to introduce myself,' I said, 'I am a man of letters and words.' And then I felt incredibly stupid for saying something like this.

'What?' She asked me, clearly not understanding what I wanted to say.

'I am a writer.' I paused for effect, and found none. Out of some social obligation she asked me, 'Got anything published? Or are you a blogger?'

I let out an audible sigh and said, 'That takes me to the tragedy that brought me here.'

'How?'

'Miss, I am but twenty three years of age, yet I was recently able to complete my first full length novel. It had taken me more than a year to write the three hundred pages, and that effort had left me emotionally drained. But I was happy with what I had written, and approaching a publisher had reaped good results.'

'So you got it published?'

'I'm coming to that. I had heard that stories get stolen when they are sent to publishers in an electronic format, so I had all the three hundred pages printed, put in a spiral binding, and I was on the way to a publisher with an office in *Hazrat Ganj*. Now it happened that…'

'That…? Then what?'

'I had a misunderstanding with the girl I loved the same morning, she had stopped returning my calls, leaving me to be pre-occupied and stressed.'

'You had a fight with your girlfriend?'

`Ha ha, Miss, she…she is not my girlfriend, she is someone who used to love me and suddenly stopped.'

'And now you will blame the girl for committing a great error, right? It's the girl who ruined your life, isn't it?'

'No, miss, I do not blame her. It was totally my fault, for the past one year I had almost completely ignored her. She was never really that committed to me, but seeing my total devotion towards her she came close to me. But I don't know why, once she started getting close, I felt like moving away from her.'

'Don't tell me. Now you are coming across as a commitment phobic guy. I believe buried in your story is some girl who cheated on you, and hence has turned you away from relationships.'

'I'll come to that later.' I said, I was interested in the perception that she was forming about me because of the tale that I was weaving. 'The day she told me that she loved me I felt that my heart was full of happiness and I needed to do something about it. That was the day I decided to let it out and write my book, wanting to write a story that culminates to the point where I had gotten the love of my life.'

'Wait...wait...all it took to start writing your whole life story was getting a girlfriend? Are you serious?'

'I wonder why that is surprising.'

'People are moved to write about their life when they feel that they have achieved something worth telling. You fell in love and you consider that your biggest achievement?'

'Miss, falling in love and finding a need to write about your own life are two different things altogether, but I believe that somehow was a trigger. I won't deny that.'

She laughed and said, 'You amuse me. You say that you are twenty-three years old, and the most significant thing that has ever happened in your life is falling in love, and yet you wrote a whole 300 page book about your life story? What did you write a page for each day of the last year of your life?'

I was slowly getting her to talk more, I was getting her to react, and I considered it a good thing because it gave me more time to think of elements of my so-called story and answering her questions added more material to it. I said, 'I never said that this was the most significant event of my life, I only said that it acted as a trigger. I have had a varied and interesting life, whatever time I had lived. And off late that girl wasn't important to me, I was drifting away from her.'

'What was her name?' The curiosity in her voice was evident.

'I can't tell a girl's name to a stranger.' I said, trying hard to contain my laughter.

There was silence from her side for some time, I strained myself trying to hear her thoughts, believing that in our present state thoughts are just words that are spoken very softly. She almost started speaking several times before conceding, 'Fine, my name is Sana…and you can call me that, no need of saying Miss all the time. Now, what was her name?'

I had succeeded in getting her to tell me her name, she was opening up to me, and now I had to think of a nice name for the girl. However, instead of dwelling on it too much, I gave her the first name that for some reason came to my mind, 'Neha', I said, 'Her name was Neha Saxena.' And now I started giving Neha Saxena a face, a voice, hobbies and habits, everything that I could think of. These details I would unleash on my present companion little by little.

From that point onwards I expanded the story ideas that I had when I was alive, and converted them to full-fledged stories for the benefit of my captive audience. I took the facets of all the love stories that I had thought of writing, for there was one thing that I had not lied to her about, I really did enjoy writing, and I connected them to tell of mine and Neha's so-called love story. I told Sana of how we met at a poetry recital in a coffee shop, and had been impressed by her beauty and intrigued by her bad poetry, which I would later find to be raw and hence extraordinarily good. I made up details about circling her house just to catch a glimpse of her ('How clichéd' Sana had commented), and how by continuously sending her poems that had nothing at all to do with her, I had made her fall in love with me.

'It seems you were pretty enamoured with her, then how come all of a sudden you thought of pushing her away from your life?'

'You'd asked me how I had started to write my story just because I found a trigger in love, well the actual reason is that I had expended a lot of time and effort in my pursuit of Neha. And once I had gotten an affirmation from her I thought of writing about it, because I really, really felt that it was something worth telling. However, once I actually did sit down to write I realized that compared to the rest of my life, this particular moment was very insignificant. I was sitting beneath the portrait of my great grandfather, who was part of the freedom struggle of our country. And I had much to write about him, and little to write about myself. That same day I took a train to Delhi where my grandfather lived. I had no idea what I wanted to do, but all I could think of was that I needed to know more about my family history, especially the contribution of my great grandfather in our country's freedom struggle.'

This time when Sana spoke the excitement in her voice was discernible, 'You mean to say that your family actually had a freedom fighter? Mr Fahad, your story has suddenly become interesting. Although by no means does it make *your* life interesting.'

I ignored that jibe and told her how I stayed with my grandfather for weeks, piecing all I could about who my great-grandfather was. In actuality both my great grandfather and my grandfather had been *vaqeels* at the Allahabad High Court. They weren't very famous, but had earned enough money for their next generation to live a life of comfort. Mentally I apologized to them for they were both dead, and here I was changing their life's story for the benefit of a stranger.

In my alternate life story my great grand-father was an adventurer who had roamed the country working with different freedom fighting groups, never as a central character but as a player whose work history had been forgotten. I reasoned this with Sana by saying that he had been always on the move, and hence couldn't find association with a single region or a single group. I made him out as someone who had continued fighting till the Quit India Movement, and who after Gandhi ji's death had decided to spend his life as a teacher in a *Madarsa* in Lucknow, imparting to students the values of love for their nation and brotherhood.

Sana listened with rapt attention while I, needing neither water to wet my throat, nor pause to rest my tongue, spoke continuously for what seemed like hours at length. I concluded the story of my great-grandfather with his fictitious death during the Emergency (where he, as an old soldier to the cause of independence, had come out of retirement and had been shot dead in one of the many unrecorded police actions during that terrible time).

Sana spoke, 'Is it all true? I mean, I hear these kind of stories, of unsung heroes who have lead such an enriched life. Now I am hearing one from a blood relative of one such hero. Thank you Farhan...'

'Er...my name is Fahad'

'Yes...sorry, thank you Fahad, for telling me this story. So this is what you had been writing for a year? I am sad that you could not get it to a publisher, I am sure that it would have been a bestseller.'

I laughed and said that what I had told her till now was only one-third of the story, I knew that I had got her hooked and that she would be eager to know the rest too.

'I have not even started on my grandfather, who lived with a non-existent father who was too devoted in his own cause and faith, while my grandfather, bless his soul, worked against all odds to study as well as to take care of his *Ammi*, and he was part of the first batch of IITians, he was a student of Kharagpur, I will tell you all about him but first...'

'First...what?'

'Miss Sana, I wish to know *your* story. Who are you, what did you do, and what unfortunate incidence brought you here.' I regretted adding the last part of the statement, but curiosity had gotten the better of me.

Sana took one of her habitual pauses and replied, 'I have not had much of a life. I got married at the age of twenty to a man whom I did not love but had grown to like. He was a good husband, but he hardly gave me any time, he worked for six days a week and was away a lot. We had been married for two years and yet he had shown no desire to start a family of our own; this had made me grow attached to the children who lived in my apartment building. And it was with one of these children that I was flying a...flying a kite on the rooftops of the apartment...and it was...it was nine floors from the...'

I heard her stifle a sob, and I cursed myself for asking her such a bad question, it would have been more prudent for me to ask her something simpler, like what her hobbies were, or who was her favourite film star.

'And...and Ravi the poor kid...no fault of his...he asked me to hold the *manji* and go back, and I went too far back... section with the weak railing and...'

'Sana...Miss! Er...no need...'

'And I was dead and still not so, and when I woke up without waking up, I could hear my poor husband cry, and he cried for many hours, and he cried until I was taken away, and even now at times I hear him crying...'

I felt bad for lying to her, for telling her an entirely made up story. I thought it would be better for me to tell her the truth, that I had a mundane life and perhaps an equally mundane death.

But then I realized that she had been happy listening to my tale, and in death I had the power of giving her this happiness,

of drowning out the voice of her husband's crying. I had enough
tales to last a life time, and an eternity to make up new ones. I
resolved to help her pass her time well by telling her my tall
tales.

The time will come to tell her about the spectacular and
important death of Mohammad Fahad, but till then I had other
stories waiting impatiently in the queue. Sana, my favourite
audience, I dedicate all my stories to you.

THE LAST ONE

Param and Krishna made their way through a garden that had been singed badly by the fires of the apocalyptic meteor shower. Param moved with a sense of predestination while Krishna followed him haplessly. They stopped in front of a square of cinder-blocks; Param said calmly, "This is where my childhood was spent. This is where the garden was...and now it's...ruined."

Krishna tried hard but couldn't evoke a feeling of sorrow, his nerves had been numbed and he was emotionally saturated, seeing the destruction of everything around him for the past few days. "Don't tell me you've come here to search for a fucking childhood toy, because you need to be with it before we die too."

"It's the end of the world," Param replied, "I am not looking for a toy; I am looking for something more important."

Krishna expected Param to step inside the remains of his house and rummage around. Instead he saw him walking towards the row of trees (or what was left of them) and get down on his knees.

"It has to be here somewhere," Param rummaged around in the mud.

"What are you looking for?"

"A sign."

"A sign? What sort of sign?"

"A sign of God."

"What? Isn't the fucking end of the world a sign from God?"

Param smirked and said, "I am looking for a cross, I put it somewhere around here as a symbol, to look for something that I'd buried around six months ago."

"What is that something?"

"I'll tell you if I find it."

Out of curiosity Krishna too started looking around for the cross, the sky was heavily overcast with ash and dust, making finding anything in the blackened mud difficult. They searched for around fifteen minutes before Krishna stumbled across a piece of wood sticking out of the ground. He pulled it out of the ground triumphantly and shouted, "I've found it!"

"No! Idiot, the thing that I'd buried was directly underneath this cross!"

Krishna stood dumbfounded for a second, then he quickly began digging around the area where he'd pulled the cross, in hope of finding what Param had hidden. He was joined by his friend, who grumbled incessantly. It took them some time as the sky above grew darker, they found a small metal box.

"Is this what you were looking for?"

Param laughed maniacally and said, "Ha ha, Yes, come let's find some shade before I open this. It might rain soon."

There were no trees with any leaves left, however, one of the trees had a very thick branch which hadn't fallen off despite the global fire. Param mentioned that this was the tree where he used to hang a tyre swing as a child.

"Do you have any battery in your cell phone?"

"No, we used it all up when we were raiding that shop last night...or day...it's too hard to tell."

"Never mind, I guess we have enough light." Param flicked open the small latch on the box, it had a cushioned lining inside and the only thing that it contained was a blue-ish bag tied at one end. He ceremoniously took the bag out, dropped his coveted box on the mud below and started fidgeting with the strings.

Inside the bag was a white card board box that Krishna too could easily identify, and it made him go wide-eyed in anticipation.

"Is that...Is that what I think it is?"

Param replied, "I can read your mind my friend, and you guessed it right, this white box contains the last cigarette on earth."

He took the cigarette out and held it aloft by the filter, as if holding a tiny sword. Krishna looked at it with childlike glee, and asked, "How...what...where did you get that?"

"I put it there, silly!"

"But...but you don't even smoke! At least not anymore!"

"I know, I quit smoking six months, two weeks and three days ago, but two weeks after that I bought one cigarette. Just one, and decided that I would smoke it only if the world comes to end. I put this clause knowing that something like this would never happen," He paused, reflecting, "Ironically, now I wish I'd thought of something else."

While Param was caught up in his thoughts, Krishna was wrestling with mixed emotions, as if he was waiting to spring on to his friend. He asked him, "What...what are you going to do with it?"

"What else! I am going to smoke it. And if you don't mind, I would rather like to smoke it alone. Haven't smoked one for the past six months, and who knows how long we have left to live."

Krishna lunged at Param and snatched the cigarette away from him. "I can't let you do this!" He said, 'You've been holding on well for the past six months, and now that the end is so close, I can't let you relapse to this dirty habit."

Param tried to take it back from him, "Fuck you! The fucking end means no more cigarettes, no smoking for anyone! I have not smoked for so long and I saved this one, I deserve this!"

Krishna replied, "Dude, think about it! Think about your resolve! You used to be an inspiration to everyone, I mean everyone who wanted to quit smoking."

Param said in a calm voice, And that "everyone" is dead.

They sat down under the branch as they heard the crack of thunder overhead. Who knew whether this rain would be acidic or would have clear water, they did not want to take the risk. Krishna held the cigarette in his hand, clutching it, but not too tightly for the fear of breaking it. He was determined to convince Param that he shouldn't be the one to smoke that cigarette, "I would be doing our friendship a great disservice if I allow you to lose your will at this point. Be strong."

"What do I gain from being strong? And I know the whole reason you are making this bullshit charade is because you want that last cigarette for yourself."

"How can you even think of such a thing? The only thing that's on my mind is to make you stop yourself from continuing this filthy habit."

"Fuck you. How the fuck am I going to continue this habit? This is the last goddamned cigarette in the entire world!"

"Well...we...we don't know that yet."

"I know that, and in my world it's the last one. Now will you please give it to me so I can smoke it and die in peace?"

Param held out his hand, Krishna hid the cigarette behind his back, and said, "No."

"No? What do you mean no? What the fuck is this no? Don't make me hit you man, give me this cigarette, why won't you give it to me?"

"I...I want to smoke it myself. It should be MY last cigarette, not yours, you had quit smoking for God's sake. You don't even need it anymore, but I do..."

"So the truth comes out, you bastard, I should have never brought you here, I knew you would have wanted it for yourself. But I brought you only because I never smoke alone. Now give me my cigarette or..."

"Or else? Or else what?"

Param was lost for words, after a while, all he could say was, "Dammit man! Why won't you give it to me? Don't you remember, I was the one who taught you to light a cigarette in the first place!"

"Yes, yes you did. You were the one who got me to start smoking, you brought in this evil habit in me, and I guess I deserve to get what I want to counter off the harm you've done to me. Don't you think so?"

"I fucking don't think so! I know I am the one who taught you to smoke, and without me you wouldn't have even known what's the difference between actually smoking and mouth fagging. You fucker, now for what I did for you, give me back my cigarette."

The two friends stared at each other, with growing hostility in their eyes. Each was waiting for the other to make the first move. "Param, you have been a good friend of mine for a long long time, that's why I am asking you nicely. Let me smoke this last cigarette, and maybe I will give you a couple of puffs."

"A couple of puffs? A fucking couple of puffs? You will give me a couple of puffs? YOU will give ME a couple of puffs? You son of a bitch, that's MY cigarette!"

"No, since the day you quit smoking no cigarette is yours, doesn't matter if you bought it, or stored it under a tree for how long, doesn't matter..."

"Like fuck it doesn't matter! Dude, right now, all that matters to me in this goddamned dying world is the fucking white stick that you are holding in your hands, and this is the last time I am warning you...remember you've never taken me down in a fist fight."

The two friends sat still, and deep within them they knew that neither had the heart or the energy to physically fight, least over a cigarette. Eventually Krishna was the one to relent, "Fuck you man, take it, if it means that much to you." And he threw the cigarette towards Param who caught it expertly.

"Of course it means a fucking lot to me," Param said, he toyed around with the cigarette in his hand, looking at Krishna who was staring into the distance. He looked at the cigarette once more, and threw it back. "Fuck this shit. It was hard for me to quit, and I'm not going to start again just because it's the end of the fucking world."

Krishna laughed and said, "Dude, our world is dying, and all we're doing is fighting over a cigarette! Ha ha, come on, for old time's sake. Let's share this."

Param smiled, "Yeah...for old times' sake."

The hostility between the two friends ceased as it started raining around them, the water splashing lightly over to their shadow spot under the branch. They picked up the cigarette from the ground which was rapidly getting wet.

Only to realize that they had no matchsticks, no lighters, nothing to light the cigarette with.

THE STREET CONJURER AND EGO

He wore a dull grey suit which would have been impressive in the past. Below the suit was a stained shirt he carefully buttoned up. He was trying to look as nice as possible while maintaining the air of a street conjurer. He performed juggling tricks and clicked small flames of evanescent fire with his fingertips. He warmed up his audience by saying, "The world claims to do magic and the world lies! There are few who remain, and can do the wonders that I do. One was my master Bhuto, and one lived on the planet Pluto, and now my master Bhuto and the planet Pluto both are no more. There is me, and only me. I am Kasif The Azam. The Great Kasif! These tricks I show, they are not by sleight of hand, no sir. I, and I alone do magic."

A thick crowd formed a circle around him, wrapping shawls, wearing sweaters and hiding themselves in the almost-solid fog. Surprisingly there was no fog in the circle in which the conjurer practiced.

He did the regular street-magician stuff, making cards and coins disappear, switching caps from the heads of the bystanders. His magic seemed mundane to me, and to a few others, but in general he was surrounded by admirers in awe.

He played several acts before taking off his dull grey hat to reveal a head with thinning hair, and then seemingly skated on shoes without wheels attached, moving in the perimeter of the circle. He said, "And now kind sirs, and more sirs because I see no madams here. It is time for interval. I shall take a five-minute rest, but please kind sirs and appreciators of True Art, I wish for a small donation, to the cause of a lost art. I, I alone am the last surviving descendant of the magicians. Please, for the sake of my forefathers and your fathers."

He got a handsome response from most of the crowd; his hat was soon full of coins, and mostly notes of the denomination of five and ten. There was also a note of fifty, given by some enthusiastic fan. When he came to me I contemplated dropping my half-smoked cigarette in his hat and watching the whole thing burn.

He stopped, his heels made a cartoonish screeching sound of brakes being applied. "Kind sir for sake of your lungs, please do not smoke. Smoking Kills --- the pack says." He produced a pack from his pocket.

"Then why do you carry a packet in your pocket?" I asked.

"This is not mine." He laughed a fat man's laugh and said, "It belongs to the gentleman on your left who I afraid shares your filthy habit." The man standing next to me quickly checked the pocket of his jeans and found that the magician was right. "Give it back!" He said, while the crowd applauded.

"What do you want sir?'

"My pack! Give it back."

"Why not sir, it is yours take it."

The man quickly took it and opened it to see its contents. "It's empty!" He cried.

"Cigarette smoking bad for health kind sir."

"But where are the cigarettes?"

The conjurer waved his hands in a strange fashion and said "May those filthy things rain upon this man, who does not know how wrong it is to smoke!" And sure enough, out of apparently nowhere, 5--6 cigarettes rained from the conjurer's hands to the ground near that man's feet. The crowd clapped again as he turned and bowed slightly to thank the crowd.

He came to me again; I kept on smoking contently until he waved his hand and doused my cigarette. I remained calm and threw away the stub. "Kind sir, for exchange of medical advice and magic tricks, a small donations, please?" He said.

I stepped up in front of him and said, "No."

"No?" He moved back to the centre of the circle and said, "why not? You do not like magic?"

"Oh I love magic, but I don't believe what you are doing counts as magic."

"Oh please sir, the display not good enough for you? You want what? Shooting stars? Cannon balls? Tell me sir, I will beg to differ and give different trick."

"What *can* you do?" I asked him.

"You challenge me sir?"

"All the things you did, that guy with a monkey in Chandni Chowk can do to. I want you to show me something very few magicians can do."

His voice turned into a menacing growl and he said, "I can kill you sir." The crowd let out a collective gasp. He changed his voice to normal and said, "I kid! I joke! I am Comedian. See, each magician has to be comedian. I make a killing joke. See?"

I moved closer to him, the crowd moved a step back, now almost afraid of the conjurer. "Can you read my mind?"

"I can do anything sir! I will prove it!" He snapped his fingers and a bowl of fire appeared in his palm, he threw it in the air and the fire turned into a crow and flew away. He was getting worked up.

"Can you read my mind?" I asked again.

"LIKE A BOOK! I am Kasif The Azam! I am no mere mortal! I know black voodoo magic of Afrika, I know white man's magic of Amrika, I have met Ashwatthama and learned magic of Mahabharat from him! Mock me do not!"

"Can you answer a question about me?" I asked.

"I know you!" He said, holding up a burning finger in front of me. "I can see your past as I can see my hand. I can see where you were and what you do now. Ask what you want I can tell what you ask."

I waited for a while to ask my question, the crowd slowly crept in closer to where the conjurer and I stood. The fire on his finger tip burnt with a constant intensity. I chose my moment and asked him, "Tell me. How much money do I have in my pocket?"

The flame on his finger jumped up to almost a foot as his eyes blazed and bore into mine. After a while the fire on his finger and his eyes died down. He said in a heavy voice, "I cannot answer that question."

The crowd looked shocked, clearly they were rooting for him to answer my question and maybe burn me using his magic. I heard distinctly audible murmurings of 'What?' and similar questions around me. "You knew I couldn't answer that question." The conjurer said, sounding so dejected that I almost felt sorry for him.

I walked away quickly, without taunting him or saying another word. I tore through the crowd, and joined my friend Prakash who was waiting for me outside the circle. He wiped perspiration from his bow and said, "Man I thought he had you there. So he wasn't really a magician, was he? Must be a big phony. I tell you my friend, it's all show, and it's all a big drama."

I smiled and said, "That man was not a phony. He was a real magician."

"What?" Prakash asked, "So how come he didn't know how much money you had in your pocket?"

"He was reading my mind, he knew what I knew."

"And?"

"And even I don't know how much money I have in my pocket."

MIRACLE DRUG

My junior was a portly fellow. He had a fat blotchy face, a bushy moustache, oily hair and a rather infectious ever present smile. Being of the variety of fat people who define the word jovial he strived to be extra helpful in spreading happiness and light all around. Thus personal space and privacy meant very little to him. He invaded your personal space both physically (being rotund) and with his incessant questions.

'Sir today also I am seeing you holding your head? Is there big, big problem sir? Work *toh* is happening smoothly sir. Any problem sir?' He would begin invariably with this gambit, and then would continue, 'Sir any health issue is there? Too much pressure you take sir! Even your moustache hair has started falling.'

I had a problem which I could not very well discuss at my work place, and especially not with my junior who spared no effort in irritating me. Besides he was a big gossip and I did not have any desire of my predicament becoming common knowledge in an office.

Not that I cared what people thought in general, but I could not think of withstanding the sea of fake sympathies that would flow towards me (mixed with hidden derision of course, along with scorn and laughter). People would laugh behind my back, '*Sahib* is stupid'.

And so when every other day my junior would trot up to me asking me why I was sitting there rubbing my temple, leaving purplish marks on my own dark forehead, and each and every time I would promptly tell him to go away without offering any explanation. Being his boss I was entitled to do this.

And being himself, he was persistent in bothering me.

'Sir, family issue sir? Want any help sir?'

And it wasn't just him, my Boss's friend in the other vertical often told him rather non-discreetly, knowing well that I sat nearby with only a thin glass wall between us, that I looked permanently sick. That my eyes betrayed a constant sleepiness and the muddy brown colour where the whites should be proved that I lived an unhealthy lifestyle.

My boss, being a genuinely good man, did not bother.

Once or twice I had heard the girl from HR commenting to someone (whispering ineffectively for my benefit) that I sleepwalked. And when I did my 9 to 6 it was quite possible that I was wide-asleep.

I hated the talk-behind-my-back. I hated mumblings and whispers made about me. I have a deep rooted belief that this world would be an infinitely better place if all people minded their own business, did their own work and left everyone else alone. I longed for a gossip-free world, a world where time was not wasted peering into someone else's life and *tsking*.

And yet, I did not lash back at anyone, except for my junior because I knew he had a genuinely thick skin and my berating him frequently had only a temporary effect on him.

A prominent reason for me not lashing back is that I have lived almost three decades carefully avoiding conflict, opting for peace instead of quarrel, contained most arguments within my head and used physical effort sparingly. I did not want to break a carefully cultivated habit. The second reason for my non-reaction (except of course in the case of my junior) was because most of what people said was true.

I was sick, in a way that only someone who was afflicted with the same disease would know.

But I wasn't always sick, these headaches weren't very old. They stayed in the background of my consciousness for quite some time. And yet in the two months since these headaches had come to the forefront and had become an almost tangible thing, they controlled and curtailed my daily existence.

I had become irritable, it had not started affecting my work but it had started affecting my peace. There always lingered the thought of something missing, of something that I was supposed to be doing and yet was not able to do. It was like an itch inside my brain which I could not cure.

One day my junior asked me if I could spare some time and accompany him somewhere. On a whim I decided not to blast him away and followed him. He took me to an empty corridor in the office and said in a soft voice, 'Sir, I have for you a headache cure. A sure cure sir.' He produced a small black polythene bag from his pocket and handed it to me.

'See sir, see please.' He prodded. I opened the bag apprehensively and saw something that looked like crushed leaves inside it. In all probability this was weed. I looked at the packet and looked back at him. The urge to slap this guy was immense. I restrained myself and asked him, in a carefully measured voice, 'Are you giving me Ganja?'

'Sir?' He seemed perplexed.

63

'Ganja! Maal! Weed! Shankar Bhagwan ka Prasad! Is this what I think it is? And are you forgetting the fact that you are trying to give me Ganja in office?'

His dark face reddened, which had the effect of making his facial hue purple. He was genuinely shocked.

'No such thing sir! This is no drug-shrug, Ram Ram.' He touched his ear lobes quickly. 'Bada Sahib you are sir, how can I commit such crime.' Then he added as an afterthought, 'Personally also sir I am not touching such kind of thing....only little bit bhang at holi, but that too once a year sir!'

I brought the packet up and smelled it, it had no discernible smell at all. 'What is it then?'

His fat man's smile returned, making his eyes squint, 'Sir this is like a family medicine. I get it all the way from Siwan. This is basically Isabgol. And my Chacha ji adds couple of other things in it to.'

'Isab...what?'

'IsabGOL sir. For jammed stomach. Constipation you are having, no?'

'What...wait...what? Where did you get that idea?'

He looked around sheepishly before speaking, 'Sir, some small marks on your forehead. Happens sir when stomach is not clean. And then odd times you use office toilet sir.'

'What? No! And...Why are you monitoring my toilet timings in office?'

His smile turned into a toothy grin, 'Only one western cistern in the entire office sir. And you yourself have given me seat near to toilet only.'

A mixture of anger and relief enveloped me; I did not know whether to laugh at this bugger or to chastise him, 'You know you really should start minding your own business.'

Almost instantly he became crestfallen, 'Why saying like this sir? I care that is why I share family cure for constipation.'

I sighed, 'I know, I know. Best interests at heart and all that. Look, I am sorry if I got angry. But I do not have constipation, and...thank you for the medicine. But you don't need to worry about me, I am okay.'

He shuffled his feet and looked down at the floor, suddenly his head shot up and said, 'Sir no harm in trying medicine. Absolutely no side effect, and Chacha ji adds something to make taste also very nice.'

I pocketed his medicine to placate him and to get rid of him. I told him that I needed to take a stroll and he should continue back in office. I mentally made a note about changing his office seat from the one near the toilet.

I walked down to the tea shop near the entrance of the company building, where thankfully a fresh bhagona of tea was being boiled. I sipped the tea and reflected that my junior was not entirely wrong. What afflicted me right now was a kind of constipation. And it affected me with the same severity as constipation might affect someone.

When I reached home that night I thought of trying again something that my friend had told me to do. I looked at the small study that I had made in the corner of my living room and saw the thick notebook and pen lying on the table. I clenched my fist, steeled my will and sat down on the chair in my study. I repeated the mantra that my friend had taught me.

'Today I will overcome my writer's block.'

And like the few other times that I had tried it before, it did absolutely nothing for me.

I opened the notebook; it was a costly thing, made out of expensive glossy paper. And it had a permanent new book smell which is one of the best smells in the world. I caressed the blank paper with my hand and gingerly picked up the black Pilot Pen. I took out my mobile phone and opened the 'memo' wherein I had noted my friend's instructions.

Stop writing on the computer, the computer is connected to Internet. The Internet is a permanent Person from Porlock (check)

Start writing the way you began writing in the first place, use your favourite pen (check)

Read a lot, and read different authors, not just your regular Crime novels (check)

When you start writing after this, tell yourself that you will overcome your writer's block (check)

Make writing a habit and not a hobby; ensure you sit down regularly to write. Discipline yourself (er...somewhat check)

Write at least 500 words each day, be prolific (.....)

I grew depressed and pushed the phone away. The white paper in front of me was alluring, and yet even with a pen in my hand I could think of nothing to write. There were no stories in my head, and the few half-baked single line ideas that I had did not have a story or characters attached to them.

It had been over ten months that I had actually completed a short story. And there were three half-complete stories clamouring for my attention. And because I had no ways and means of completing them, no end in sight, I avoided them. I was afraid of destroying good ideas and I was afraid of creating bilge.

What had once been my favourite pastime had now become a strenuous exercise. And it made me feel impotent. Words once had flown naturally from my fingers, and I was quite proud of my own turn of phrase. But over a period of time my output had decreased. It was not a sudden thing. First the average length of my stories came down from 5000 words to 2500 words. Then the gap between two stories increased from being a month to being two months and more. I used to execute my ideas within three to four months (queued up as they were, I would pick them one by one and finish them off), right now I had ideas lying with me for more than a couple of years and yet I had no strength, no inspiration or imagination to convert them to stories.

The discomfort started as a nagging feeling some six months ago. It felt like there was something I was supposed to do but I wasn't doing it, or something that I had forgotten to do, like turn off the stove before stepping out of the house. This nagging feeling soon started turning into actual physical agony.

To counter this I started spending a lot of time on the Internet, trying to divert my mind using list based humour sites and watching a string of YouTube videos. This helped for a while, but in the long run it had a counter-effect. It actually took me even further away from writing, so that now even when I felt compelled to write I had these distractions to stop me from doing so.

It had gotten worse. The thought that it was almost a year since I last completed a story depressed me, and it was something I could not share with any one at my workplace. No one there even knew that I wrote stories, nor did I think anyone would care. So when people tended to ask me what the reason for my sour mood was, I found no fitting reply.

I sought intervention from a writer friend who gave me the above mantra around a month ago. He chided me for being an idiot, told me that I needed a swift kick to get me started and said that the basic thing for me was to bring discipline in my life. Writing would follow.

For a month I heeded his advice unsuccessfully. I read a lot of varied fiction, I even read the masters like King and Bradbury's notes on writing. More or less all the prolific authors had the same thing to say as my friend, and this made me think that I was at least on the right track even though I had not started writing in actuality.

And today, when I once again stared blankly at the page in front of me, I came close to crying. I scribbled a few lines on the page, read them, scratched them out violently, capped the pen, closed the note book and covered my face with my palms.

A couple of days later I decided to humour myself by telling my concerned junior about my predicament. I knew full well that he would not even understand what I was so bothered about, especially because it was neither a work-related nor a health-related problem. We were sitting in a small cafeteria near our office and he asked me if the medicine was working. I instead told him what the real problem was, he listened intently for a while and tried to check whether I was actually joking or not.

'Sir but many people don't write stories. I also don't write. I have no headache. How this happen sir?'

I tried to explain, 'Because I like writing stories, and suddenly I find it impossible to write them. Tell me, if there was something that you liked doing a lot and after sometime weren't unable to do so, wouldn't you be troubled like me?'

He toyed with the half-eaten samosa lying on his plate, silently contemplating what I had just told him. 'I understand sir.'

'Of course you do....wait a minute, you do?'

'Sir,' he said, 'I like eating paan. You also know sir, daily five paan I have to eat else day doesn't go well. Now if someday it happens that I do not get paan then I become very uncomfortable sir. And imagine not eating paan for ten months! Life would be absolutely bad sir. Hey Raam, Shiv Shiv.'

I did not like it that he equated my story writing to his paan chewing habit, but on the base level he was right. This bastard never managed to stop surprising me, I had not put it up to him to understand my problem. And yet, even though a bit crudely, he had pointed out the crux of the matter.

He sipped his frooti noisily and said, 'In this problem sir Chacha Ji medicine cannot help.'

'No. It most definitely will not. Do you want it back?'

He looked appalled, 'No sir! It is a gift. Giving gifts back brings bad luck both to receiver and giver. You want more bad luck sir?'

'Not at all. Just a suggestion, never mind. Anyway, the thing is, now that you know my problem I think you understand that it is something that you might not be able to help me out with. Do you agree?'

'Not totally agreeing sir. Because all problems have solutions, and for your problems I am solution.'

There was no getting away from this guy. 'Look, don't worry too much okay? I think I will be able to manage...'

'You are manager sir. Of course you will manage.' He laughed. 'I am on your case sir. This problem also I will solve.'

I muttered several obscenities under my breath, mostly directed towards myself. I faked a smile and said thanks.

For a week my junior did not bother me at all. I hoped against hope that he had forgotten about me and perhaps someone else's malady would have gotten him more interested. There were people who would have been nursing problems more serious compared to mine, and I would not have minded it at all if he attached his helpfulness elsewhere.

But, I was wrong.

Exactly a week after that time in the cafeteria he came up to me and again asked me to accompany him to that empty corridor. I suspected another medicine from his Siwan wale

Chacha ji when I saw him digging deep in his trouser pocket. Instead, he produced a crumpled pamphlet. He gave it to me to read while his smile beamed in contrast to his face.

'Read sir. Read. Very nice solution I have got.'

The pamphlet was similar to advertisements that I had seen in local trains. It was an ad for a clinic run by Baba Haqeem Usmani who claimed to solve most problems of the world, which included (but were not limited to) piles, erectile dysfunction, low sperm count, tension in family, property disputes, lack of luck in love and financial issues. The Baba also provided loans with minimum guarantee documents.

I read the pamphlet twice and flipped the page to make sure that I wasn't missing anything. Then I asked the junior in my coldest voice possible, 'What is the meaning of this?'

'Sir please to listen first sir. Very effective this Baba is. I have also gone there once for....some personal problem. Never mind sir, but believe me. This Baba will help.'

'This? This Baba....This is worse than your Kayam Churn...'

'Isabgol sir...'

'Whatever! Do you think that I would debase myself by going to such a fake medicine man? Do you think I would actually consider going to one of these pile cure centres? Are you out of your mind?'

This time despite my verbal abuse his sheepish grin did not lose his face, 'Sir I have already discussed your problem with the Baba ji. He says he has a solution.'

It was one of those things which you do on a whim, one of those decisions that you know you would immediately regret. And yet I saw myself standing in front of a depilated building in one of the older parts of the city. Standing in front of me was my junior, grinning like he always did. The door to the building was unhinged and the entire structure felt like it would not survive another monsoon.

'I have a bad feeling about this.' I said.

'No more of bad feelings sir! All bad feeling go away after this. You will be completely new. Come sir.' He led me inside the building, pushing at the door confidently. We climbed three and a half flights of stairs which took us to a mezzanine floor with a hole in the wall structure. I was expecting a Baba wearing long robes, sitting on the floor in a dingy room somewhere. Sitting in front of me was a very normal looking bespectacled old man wearing a striped shirt and muddy brown trousers. His office/ shop was beneath the slope of the stairs, and he had a small stool, a table and a table fan. There were two metal chairs near his table. He looked at my junior, smiled, and motioned us to sit on the chairs. My junior insisted that I take the seat nearer to the table. With some trepidation, I did.

My junior spoke, 'Babaji this is my boss I had told you about. Special problem.'

He looked at us genially, 'Yes, yes. Erectile dysfunction, isn't it? Often leads to problem at home. But I have perfect...'

I interjected quickly, 'Wait, no. That is not...' I turned to my junior, 'What did you tell him the problem was?'

My junior was as shocked as I was, his face did the purple colouring thing again, 'No no Baba. You must be confused. Not erection problem. Mind problem.'

The man had a quizzical look on his face, but it was quickly replaced with a benevolent smile. 'Memory loss? Just the thing. You will remember everything like it was yesterday.'

My junior grew almost hysterical, 'No no Baba ji. Not memory problem. Writing problem!' Saying this he made a writing gesture in the air.

'Oh...achcha. Bad handwriting. Bachcha sadly no definite cure for that. Only in your next life will you have better handwriting, I can see it written on your forehead.'

I was frustrated by now, I silenced my about-to-speak junior with a hand and said, 'Baba ji, I don't know what this oaf has told you or not told you. And I don't know whether you will have a solution for my problem. Still since I have come thus far I will tell you what it is.'

And then I proceeded to narrate my problem to him, because once you are in to participating in a farce it is always better to carry it through and close it. While I told him about my earlier capacity for churning out stories and filled in small anecdotes about the time since it had started going downhill, he meticulously made notes in calligraphic Arabic script. He asked me at times to repeat what I had told him and then when I was done he kept his pen down and cracked his fingers.

He sat in deep thought for a while. He opened a drawer and took out several small notebooks, he consulted them for almost fifteen minutes, skimming each one and discarding them until his face visibly brightened up as he found out what he was looking for. He copied something down on the note pad in front of him and then swept all the small notebooks back in the drawer.

'Son,' he said, 'this is a rare problem because very few have the courage to bring it up. I will not brag to you but I have had a couple of famous film writers come here a few years ago and they told me that they too faced something similar. In fact other kinds of artists too have come...it is not a medical disease, all you need to do is unlock your brain.'

He paused for effect and waited for us to fill the gap with a probing question, 'And how do I unlock my brain Baba ji?'

'Fortunately I have the key. Unfortunately I do not have it with me right now. Come back a week later, I will have the medicine ready. My fees will be fifteen thousand one hundred and fifty-one rupees only.'

'What? How much?'

'Son, the medicine for this is very rare and very costly. Fortunately I have friends in such places who can get it for me. The medicine that exists contains one-tenth of a drop of ink used in the writing of the actual Kathasaritsagar.'

I stared at him in disbelief, 'You are joking.' I said.

'No I am not. Pay me after you write your first story.'

'Kathasaritsagar....really?'

The man smiled and nodded. 'As I said, it is very rare. And you don't need to pay me upfront. Use the medicine and pay me after you end up writing the first story.'

Heat and dust welcomed us as I rushed out of the building. 'What a complete...' before I could use an expletive my junior stopped me, 'Impressive Baba ji sir. Not fraud, hundred percent effective. I speak from personal experience.'

I hailed a Black-Yellow taxi and before my junior could follow me inside it I slammed the door shut. 'Not a word about this to anyone. And this matter is closed. I hope I have made myself clear.' And then I brusquely told the taxi driver to drive on.

For seven days my junior avoided me completely, he shirked out of sight as soon as he saw me and I too did not call him for any work, choosing instead to pass on any message using the network of other office underlings.

However, I was not surprised when on the eighth day he promptly turned up on my desk with his goofy grin in place. 'Sir, please don't be angry.' He said, and he placed a small vial on my table. It was like one of those mini bottles which are used to sell homeopathic medicines.

Even though I knew the answer, I asked him, 'What is this? More importantly, what is the meaning of this?'

'He he he, sir. Please don't be angry.' He then produced a square piece of paper from his pocket. I picked it up and saw instructions written in Hindi.

Mix one drop in a glass of warm water and drink exactly at 10 PM in the night.

Do not drink more than three drops at a single time.

Do not mix with milk, tea, alcohol or anything else apart from water.

Do not eat anything for at least half an hour after taking the medicine.

Do not drink more than once a day, however, can be drunk daily.

If you face any side effects like nausea, vomiting, loose motions, please immediately call on the number below.

And below the numbered instructions was a note saying that after writing the first story payment should be made at the same place and in cash.

'I admire your guts you know.' I said, 'you have the cheek to go behind my back even though I told you not...'

'Sir, please try no sir. What harm is there?'

'You imbecile, you bloody nincompoop. How dare you?' I tried to fill in as much anger as I could in my voice without raising it, I did not want to create a scene in the office. 'Get away from here before I slap your teeth out.'

He was resolute, neither his grin nor he moved from his place. 'Sir, seriously. There is no harm. Please try no.'

'You....you have crossed all limits!' I clenched my fists, and breathed deeply. 'I will....I can fire you, do you know that?'

'No sir.' He smiled, 'At least not today. I am on leave today sir. Leave for three days sir. You approved yesterday sir. On email.'

And he suddenly turned on his heels as quickly as his portly frame allowed him to do so, and then he walked away from the office briskly.

I counted slowly till six hundred, making sure that ten minutes had passed. Then I picked up the vial to throw it away. Curiosity got the better of me and I opened the bottle and sniffed it. It had a pleasant sweet-sour smell. And then I sighed, put the vial in a small pocket of my laptop bag and cursed my junior. His concern was both touching and irritating, and somehow I did not want to let his insolence and effort go to waste.

I kept the vial on my study, adding it to the list of things that should compel me to write. In hindsight I looked at the entire incident in a humorous light. I thought that I should write a story keeping my junior as a central character, a bumbling do-gooder who does more harm than good. With this sudden inspiration I immediately sat down to write the story. I was happy, and I wanted to start with a killer opening line.

And then words failed me. Words literally failed me.

I had no control over the next chain of events. I walked to the kitchen and heated a glass of water, put it in a glass tumbler, opened the small bottle, roughly measured a drop in the cap and poured it in the glass. The blackish drop quickly dissolved and made no impact on the colour of the water. I drank the entire glass in one shot. The water had no taste whatsoever. Then I said to myself, 'Kathasaritsagar...huh!'

After a few minutes a slight drowsiness overcame me. I went and sat on my beanbag and fell into the sweet spot between sleep and wakefulness. When I woke up I saw that exactly thirty minutes had passed. I felt a slight buzzing in my head, like the onset of one of my regular headaches. The nerve on the right side of my head throbbed and it felt like a taut bass guitar string. I tried to massage it but it felt very raw, and then suddenly, something exploded inside my brain.

I rushed to my study and attacked the page with a violence I did not know I was capable off. If I was in an animated cartoon show then there would have been smoke coming out of the nib of my pen. I had begun to write a story after a long long time. I started with

'It was a bright and sunny day...'

I did not realize that I hadn't left my seat for about an hour, nor had I stopped writing in that period. I had filled over six pages with a flowing story. I took a break to review it and count the number of words. I had ended up writing eighteen hundred words, more than what I had written in the entire year before this day. I was happy, I was emotional, and the best part was that I was not done yet. I yearned to write more.

I got up, stretched my legs and got a bottle of water from the fridge for myself. And then with a 'Bismillah' on my lips I started writing again.

I wrote for the better part of the night, it was the most I had written in a single sitting. I slowed down a bit as the hours went by but I continued writing, more or less satisfied with what I had written so far.

By four o'clock in the morning I had the first draft of an entire story ready with me. I was exhausted and tired, but I was happily tired. I sent an SMS to my boss stating that I was not well and would not be able to come to the office that day, I wrote about having a stomach infection because that boded the least amount of query from office.

And then I slept. I slept with a peace that I hadn't known for close to a year now. I slept a comfortable and dreamless sleep so that when I woke up automatically around noon I was completely refreshed.

My elation gave way to doubt a couple of days later. I had no proof that it was the medicine that had made me write. And because I was so satisfied with having completed one story (I had typed it up and mailed it to my friend who told me it was a good tale and that I was on my way back to form) I had no intention of writing another quickly. Doubt crept in. I figured it was perhaps due to mental stress, fatigue and a late effect of my friend's mantra. I did not want to believe that some medicine given to me by an obviously fraud Baba had cured my writer's block. And yet some part of me wanted to believe that I had found a cure, a miracle drug, and now I could write away at will.

And yet, I decided that I would pay the Baba the ridiculous fee that he was charging, and consider it as a treat that I had given myself for coming back to writing (which was in many ways like coming back to life). I did not let on to my junior what had transpired but I gave him the cash and told him that whenever possible he should go and give the fees because even though the vial might have been worthless it would have cost the Baba something, and thus he deserved to get some money.

That weekend I was careful not to drink any alcohol. I wanted to test the Baba's medicine one more time. I looked at the notebook lying in almost exactly the same position that I had left it after completing the story and transferring it to MS Word, at ten o'clock I had another drop of the medicine in warm water. This time I patiently waited for the effects. The drowsiness did not get repeated in the same intensity, and yet I was having a feeling of déjà vu. Almost everything happened the same way, at ten thirty I got up involuntarily and started writing.

'Jay Saxena was a homeless man with a one crore cash deposit in a bank account in....'

After the first paragraph I paused. I was writing a story with the central idea that I had nursed for around two years. And then I continued writing. This time I had a bottle of water and a pack of Parle-G biscuits lying on the table so that I would not need to take a break from writing.

It was a good thing that the next day was a Sunday, because I wrote continuously till four o'clock. And when I finished, my fingers were tired and sore but I had a six-thousand word story written out in front of me. And with one old idea executed I felt that the burden of not writing for all these months reduced somewhat.

The entire week I remained in a happy mood, eagerly waiting for the next weekend to come. Even now some cynical part of me wanted to say that this was some fluke, but broadly I was happy. I reasoned that the drug might be just a placebo, yet if it was making me write from my own volition that there was nothing to complain about.

The people in my office saw this change in my attitude, I did not snap at everyone, I even treated my junior kindly and when my boss started shouting at me once I did not shout back like I usually did, instead I listened politely and then gave him a calm and measured response. This one eighty degree turn in me confused my boss and my co-workers. So much that on Thursday over coffee my boss asked me quite directly, 'What has gotten into you? One day you are biting everyone's head off and these days you are acting like a total Santa Claus. Why are you so happy? Some girl-shirl in life?'

I told my boss that if that was the case he would be the first person to know, I was on the verge of telling him about how I had overcome my writer's block but I did not expect him to understand. So I kept mum and instead said that I had started watching 'Art of Living' and 'Baba Ramdev' videos on YouTube, and was slowly understanding the futility of anger.

'Well, good for you.' He told me with a scowl, not properly believing whether what I was telling him was the truth.

On my third experiment with the drug on a Friday night (when for the second week running I told my friends that it wasn't possible for me to join them) I decided that I would let the third time decide. If it worked this time again then there would definitely be something in the drug which was boosting my writing.

This time I kept my mind blank, banking on stumbling upon an entirely new story. This would also help me check whether it was actually the Baba's drug which was helping me write or whether I had suddenly developed a very fertile imagination.

I numbed my mind with an hour of mindless YouTube videos from nine to ten, and then at the exact strike of the hour I took my medicine. I thought of going back to watching YouTube for another half hour but then decided against it, and rested my eyes for the duration.

At ten thirty I found myself at my desk again, I evoked Monty Python and said, 'And now for something completely different.' I took inspiration from the alarm clock lying on my table and started writing a story about an alarm clock which told its owner when to be 'alarmed'. It was a funny story and I finished writing in four hours. My speed of writing had increased and this was the first time that I had written a story about a completely new idea and executed it in a single sitting.

They say that the third time is the charm (or words to the effect), I was convinced that this medicine was something special, it was working and it was making me happy.

I set myself in a routine, every Friday I would write a story after taking a drop of the drug. For a few weeks I was content with this set routine, however, soon something peculiar started happening. The headaches returned.

This time the headaches were not because I was not able to write stories, it was because I wanted to write as frequently and as much as possible. I used to wait for every Friday with a feverish desperation, doing my best to not consume the drug on other weekdays knowing it would play havoc with my timings and would lead to problems in the office. But my resolve started weakening as time went by. By Friday of each week I used to literally shake and sweat as I tried to control myself till 10 in the night.

On the plus side my stack of stories was growing and my friend had started looking for a publisher on my behalf considering my suddenly industrious output, but the flipside of it was that I felt different, and not better. It was now as if someone else was writing the stories, and the comfort of telling these tales was replaced with compulsion.

On one particular Friday I decided I would not take the drug and went to watch a Nine-to-Twelve show of a movie instead. I lasted till eleven o'clock, post which I left the movie in between and rushed home to take the drug again.

Once I tried breaking the habit, I took an advance mid-week leave on Thursday and consumed the drug on Wednesday night. It changed nothing. I wrote a story on Wednesday but on Friday I had the craving again, worse still the next Wednesday it became very hard for me to stop myself from taking the drug.

Within a span of three months I had cleared away all the backlog of my mind, all the ideas I had filed away for future were over. It was a major achievement for me since I had managed to revive a lot of stories that I thought were relegated irreversibly to the graveyard of untold tales, and as I had finished writing the final word of the final old idea I was positively drained. It was a pleasant exhaustion, similar to that experienced by marathon runners after they complete a race or by mountain climbers once they reach their summit.

'No more.' I said to myself, and then involuntarily added, 'please.'

That day I counted the number of stories that I had written, compiled them in a word document and mailed it across to my friend. I took the notebook and locked it in a drawer, post which I was careless with the key. I took the vial and tried to bring myself to empty its contents in the sink, but I found that I was unable to do so.

I decided that I would deal with it the next day, and slept. That day I slept for almost fifteen hours so when I woke up it was evening again. I ate a light snack to energize myself and then slid the vial down my jeans pocket. I walked to the small open *naala* about a kilometre from my house to give the vial a watery grave. I closed my fist around the small bottle and swung it towards the water, to my surprise when I opened my fist I found that the vial was still in my hand. I tried a few more times but could not bring myself to throw it away.

I left the bottle on a small platform near the *naala* and walked away quickly, only to run back and pocket it again. I came back home, defeated.

The ensuing week was the worst that I had ever had. Since my mind was completely blank and no old ideas existed there was something inside my brain which kept on telling me that I need to take a drop of the drug as soon as possible because I needed a new idea. I kept temptation at bay by staying in office and working till late each day, but I worked ineffectively. I could hardly concentrate on the excel sheets swimming in front of me, and all I wanted to do was to rush home and take a drop and start writing. I started doing other things to resist the craving. I ate a lot of food to make myself sluggish, I doodled on blank pages to while away time, I devoured obscure Wikipedia articles by the bucketful, and all this helped me get through till Friday.

On Friday like clockwork I lost self-control. I took a drop and churned out another short story. This time the story was nowhere close to any kind of idea that I had ever written. It was a good story and in other circumstances I would have been very satisfied with the output. Instead, I was horrified. This was not my story, and I could not take any pride in having written it.

I called up my boss the next morning and asked for a week's worth of privilege leave.

'What? All of a sudden? You do realize that you need to inform me at least a month prior to taking such a long leave. This throws a spanner in all my plans.'

'Sorry boss, the tickets and everything have already been booked; in fact I booked those around six months ago. It is a very important trip with my friends, boss. I had actually told you about this. Remember that day at that party...'

'Did you?' My boss paused and thought for a while, trying to recollect whether I had actually taken his permission,' 'Well... damn you! Go. But at least give me a reminder or a notice the next time around.'

I wanted to get away from my house, I booked a flight to my friend's city and informed him that I was coming over for a week. I told him that he did not need to take a leave, I would stay at his home and I was doing this only because I needed a change in scenery.

It was very hard for me, but I left the vial behind. I managed this by deciding not to take any luggage with me at all, not even my laptop. All I had with me was my phone and my wallet. I decided I would buy fresh clothes once I reached my friend's place.

I stayed there leading a decidedly sedentary lifestyle. I ordered and ate junk food, read crime novels by Surendra Mohan Pathak, drank beer for breakfast and caught afternoon shows for different movies every afternoon. In the evenings I spent the time drinking old monk with water and going through all the stories that I had written till now with my friend and correcting them for grammar and marking down places where I needed to improve them.

I did not tell my friend about the drug, partly because he was very proud of me being on a writing spree and I did not want to share credit for that with a medicine, and partly because I doubted whether he would believe in the existence of such a medicine. I was sure that like I had done initially, he would write it off as a placebo and tell me that all the stories were already in my head.

But there were no more stories left. My head felt curiously blank in that department. What remained was a desire to take that drug again and write some more.

On the last day of my stay at my friend's place I tried to see whether I still needed the drug. I borrowed an elaborate idea from my friend and sat down to write a story on it. I wrote a couple of paragraphs, and then scratched them out. I wrote a couple of pages and then crumpled them up and threw them away. I wrote another couple of pages and when I read them I was thoroughly disgusted by how morose and boring the tale was coming up. I tore it all up and did not make another attempt at writing.

When I finally left my friend's house I was in a very bad shape, I was facing withdrawal symptoms, had become both sad and irritable and thus had left my friend really worried. He saw me off with a plea to either see a doctor or get married or quit the job and find a new one in this city. I smiled weakly and promised that I would do all three things.

I dreaded reaching my home, I was shivering with anticipation all the way back. Even the cab driver offered me a paracetamol thinking that I had caught a cold and fever.

As soon as I reached home the first thing that I did was take my notebook out from the drawer and set it back on the table, then I retrieved the vial from the kitchen cabinet and put it next to the notebook. The time then was eight o'clock in the evening. For two hours straight I sat on the beanbag while staring at the table. And as soon as the clock struck ten I went through the motions.

The next morning I woke up disgusted with myself, appalled at my lack of self-control and at how my habit of taking the drug had moved further from the need of writing a story to just taking the drug and in compulsion writing a story. My attempt the week before had taught me that I could not get rid of the drug by throwing the vial away or leaving it somewhere. I got up and tried to flush it away in the washroom but again found myself unable to do so.

I was one step away from calling up a rehab clinic and committing myself to confinement. It was time for me to take drastic action. The first thing I did was to break the timing. I took a drop of the drug in the morning, and I was surprised to find out that I was able to do so. It lead me to write a very short story, this perhaps meant that the drug had a lower effect in the morning than nights.

The second thing I decided was that since the only way I could wean myself off the curse of this vial was by consuming it as quickly as possible. So as soon as I finished writing the short story I immediately took another drop, this time increasing the quantity of the drug. I do not remember the time it took for to write the next story because all I was waiting for was to finish and take some more of the drug.

The next time I took the vial (which was around a fourth of the total original quantity) and forced myself to empty it in the glass of water. Even now the drug dissolved completely and the colour of the water did not change. I closed my eyes and drank the mixture as quickly as I could.

And then I went completely blank.

The next thing I remember is waking up in the middle of the day to bright sunlight hitting my face. I half-expected to wake up with a searing headache, instead what I had was a fantastically unbearable light headedness. My mind was free. On instinct I picked up my digital watch which was lying on the side table next to the bed. The time was twelve o'clock in the afternoon. The date was however two days ahead of what my mind thought it should be.

To crosscheck I searched for my cell phone, I saw it lying on the ground next to the bed. It was completely discharged. I plugged it in charging and switched it on. To my horror the date that I was seeing on the watch was confirmed. I had taken the drug on Saturday. And I had woken up on Tuesday.

There were a few missed calls of my boss. I quickly called him up and after he finished shouting at me for not answering phone calls and not responding to his emails I quickly responded by saying that I had fallen hopelessly sick on vacation and was under heavy medication. My boss said that being hungover did not count as being under heavy medication. He told me to see him first thing the next day. I pushed it away as a problem to be dealt with later.

I was feeling the best that I had ever felt in days with the only pain point being that I felt very very hungry, since I had literally not eaten for two days. And I knew that the worst that my boss would do was severely reprimand me, all I needed was to be apologetic and make sure I worked hard for the next couple of weeks. I was in an impossibly good mood and decided to treat myself by cooking an old-style breakfast of toasted bread, eggs and cornflakes.

It was perhaps because I was in such an elated mood that I failed to realize the horror around me.

Until the time that I was cooking breakfast and sat down to eat it, I was totally oblivious to my surroundings. As soon as I took the first bite of scrambled eggs and toast the realization of what was around me hit, and it hit hard.

There was writing on the bed sheet, barely intelligible writing but writing nonetheless. I stopped eating and picked up the bed sheet to see it completely covered with words. I immediately started searching for the notebook, I found it lying on the study. I flipped its pages to see that I had filled it completely. And then I saw that across the house there were pages strewn around, I had written on every blank page that was around, and when they had gotten over I had written in the margins of old newspapers. When the newspapers had gotten over I had written on the blank side of all the take-away menus that I had collected over the years. And when I had ran out of those I had attacked my white bed sheet and covered it with ink.

Something subconsciously had prevented me from spoiling my book collection, the books' margins and blank pages were safe, but every other surface where writing was possible had been written upon. I saw failed attempts of writing on the wall near my bed, but thankfully the walls had expensive laminate paint which made it impossible for me to write on it. The floor too being completely tiled was protected. I surmised that I had stopped writing after I had either ran out of places to write on or had lost the energy to go on.

I was thankful that I over the past few weeks I had formed a habit of locking away my laptop in my office drawer, otherwise it would have given my drug induced self a near unlimited supply of writing material.

I packed everything that I could of the strewn about pages, the newspapers and the bed sheet and put it inside a small steel trunk that I had. My first impulse was to lock it up and burn it at some desolate place, but after thinking for some time I decided to courier it lock-stock to my friend and then later decide what to do with it eventually.

I took all the pens in the house and put them in the dust bin. I saw the empty vial lying on the floor, I touched it gingerly with my foot and then kicked it away.

I stepped into the washroom and almost shouted when I saw my reflection in the mirror. My skin looked thinner than it had been a couple of days ago, and there was blood caked under my nostrils and at the corner of my eyes. There were dark circles under both my eyes like I had been punched twice. I took a long shower trying my best to not think about the horror I had narrowly escaped.

The pain came later. It crept upon slowly without warning. After setting the house in order as best as I could I ordered and ate a copious amount of dal khichdi and then I slept once again. When I woke up I felt my entire left hand paining in every joint right from the tip of the fingers to the shoulder blade. The fingers in particular were affected the worst. I could hardly move them. Having the left over dal khichdi for dinner was a very arduous task. I wept as I felt the sudden emptiness. I wept as the magnitude of what I had escaped dawned upon me. And after the pain and tears came a surge of relief, which threatened to knock me down. For the third time in twenty four hours, I lay down to sleep.

The next day I re-joined office and handled my boss' anger. I saw my junior and thought that I should call and berate him because it was quite possible that he was the root cause of all my misery. But I let go, because I wanted to be decoupled from this entire episode of my life, and confronting him (or the Baba who had sold me the drug in the first place) would have meant prolonging it.

Strangely, the urge to write and the discomfort from not being able to write were both completely gone. It was like I had undergone an operation. Something was removed from my body, and now I was a different person altogether. Writing no longer remained a habit.

It has been a year since I stopped writing. And it seems like I never wrote at all. My friend has found an editor and he is trying to improve my stories and get them published. I have told him to use a pseudonym since I do not want to have anything to do with my stories now. The trunk full of two days of binge writing is in a corner of his house. It is locked and at my behest he has not opened it till now. I will see what to do with it once I gather courage.

These days I have found a relatively innocuous habit. I have taken up painting. I find it a lot safer. I am sure it will not take me to the brink of madness.

And I have decided to steer away from any kind of help offered by my junior for the rest of my life.

ETERNAL RETURN

Every time they met it was on the same day, and on a fixed hour, to the dot of the minute. It was on a bridge over the longest river in the country, and it was one of their favourite spots when they were still a couple. The boy always wore a slightly torn brown jacket, and the girl a green sweatshirt. The boy had a notebook in his hand which despite the years that had passed was in good condition, the girl always brought her backpack. Filled with exactly the same content every time they met.

"You look...lovely." The boy said.

"And you look the same as always. Did you take a bath?" The girl asked him.

The boy was annoyed, "What does taking a bath have to do with anything? Do I ever ask you how often or for how long do you have your blasted baths?"

The girl pretended to be angry and said, "Until you take a bath I am not going anywhere!"

"Well I already was in the mood of not going anywhere, so I guess yeah...we both agree."

They stood in silence, watching the few boats that moved lazily around the river. The boy, as always, relented first, "Okay okay, I took a bath before coming. Happy?"

The girl chuckled and said, "You know I love teasing you so much..."

A shadow crossed over the boys' face, and he said, "...used to..."

"Used to what?"

"Used to love teasing me, it was all so long ago."

The girl felt sad too, at first she tried arguing with him, "Look, it isn't exactly my fault that things are the way they are." The boy responded by growing sadder, she tried to cheer him up, "Forget about the past, concentrate on the present *na!* We are together, see!"

The boy looked at his watch and said, "We are together for precisely twenty-seven minutes more."

The girl asked him, "You have a choice, do you want to spend these twenty-seven minutes.."

"...twenty-six and half..."

"Shut up! Whatever time is left, do you want to spend it being sad or being happy? We won't be meeting for another year after this, and you know that."

The girl moved closer to the boy and tried to put her hand on his shoulder. The boy moved away sharply and said, "Don't try to touch me!" He saw the crestfallen look on her face, "I am sorry dear. Please, remember what happened the last time. We need to remain the way we are."

They returned to their boat gazing, the boy kept his notebook on the railing of the bridge and slowly turned its pages without any sense of purpose, while the girl removed a hair clip from her bag and started trying different permutations and combination in tying her hair.

This time it was the girl who spoke, in a dejected voice, Why do we always keep coming back to this place? Why do we keep on having the same conversation over and over again? Why...after all these years since..."

The boy snarled and said, "Was that a real question or a rhetorical one?"

The girl shrugged, "Whatever."

He swept his hands up dramatically, "I believe we keep on coming back here because of Nietzsche."

The girl looked at him, perplexed, "How does your stupid Nietzsche come into the picture?"

"Well Nietzsche gave the concept of Eternal Recurrence, by which, we are doomed to meet here year after year, at the same time, and have the same conversation always." He laughed.

The girl too smiled, "You and your stupid Nietzsche, did you even read any of his works when we were..." She stopped, too weak to finish her sentence.

The boy turned to her and said, "You want to know why I am always in such a foul mood?"

He waited for the girl to react and said, "You don't even know how happy I am to see you..."

"You don't look happy..."

"Yes! And it's not because of you, it's because of this bloody time limit that we have," he checked his watch again, "Less than seven minutes now! This! This is what drives me mad, this is what angers me, that the time I get to spend with you is so less."

The girl started crying, invisible tears streaking down her face. She mumbled *I love you* in a choked voice.

The boy saw that clearly things were going out of control, "Dear! Please don't cry! Wait, okay no more sad talk! We will be happy for the limited time that we have together, heck, I won't even check the time." Saying this, he took off his wrist watch and threw it in the water.

The girl stared at him, shocked.

"See," the boy said, "Time doesn't matter now! Ha ha! Err...what's wrong?"

"Fool! I had gifted you that wrist watch!"

They wasted a couple more minutes in silence, the girl used all her will power to suppress her anger and said, "It's okay. It was just a wrist watch, there will be another."

The boy cautiously showed optimism, "Yes. A brand new wrist watch, for a brand new year."

"You will be back here next year too *na?*" The girl asked, with hope in her voice.

"As always," the boy said, and as an afterthought added, "I love you."

"Love you too. I am sorry that we are dead."

"I am sorry too dear...but there is literally nothing we can do about it, can we?" The boy laughed nervously.

They waited until their time together was almost up. Then they bade each other farewell, knowing that they are bound to return at the same spot the next year, on the anniversary of their death. And they left neither happy, nor sad, knowing that they are eternally bound to each other, and that there is neither gratification, nor an escape.

THE FLYING MOUNTAIN

All the birds flew away, except one.

She was sleeping quite comfortably in her nest, and her partner had often told her that it would take an earthquake to wake her up from her slumber.

Apparently it took something more than that.

The troubles that love put him in made him think many times over whether it was all worth it, whether he had been better off living with his seven brothers, attempting the flying formation, and roaming across the green without any shackles.

And yet, he persisted with his love. He felt that it was a thankless job, but some part of him said that for the effort that he had already expended in this love story, he needed to continue. He needed to persevere for all that to mean something.

He always grumbled about love, and today he was grumbling more than usual because he was presently holding in his beak a rare and beautiful flower. It was a flower which had been described to her by a friend of hers (he would have gleefully wringed that friend's neck if he had known in advance the trouble that he would have to face to get this flower), and she had insisted that to prove (for the tenth, or maybe eleventh time) his undying devotion towards her, he should get her this flower as soon as possible.

It was as simple as plucking a wild flower from a bush, except that this time the bush grew on a place called '*Makardweep*', quite literally---alligator island.

He had expected the island to be shaped like an alligator, he had also expected that even if there were alligators on the island, the land area would be big enough for him to quickly dive down, pluck the flower and be on his way.

What he had not known was that the island was not exactly an island, it was more of a small stretch of land in the middle of a lake. And it got its name not from its shape but from the chief inhabitants who lay there in a swarm, basking away in the sunlight, with their mouths open to trap poor unsuspecting birds like him.

What he had also not known was that the island was an excruciating half day of continuous flying towards the east away from his hill.

Once he had caught sight of the nightmare that awaited him in the middle of the lake, he had a good mind to abort the mission, go back and tell her that the flower cannot be brought without exchanging it for a wing or half a body, and that if she wanted the flower she should bloody well go get it herself.

But then he imagined the tantrum, anger and tears that would follow, along with the regular taunts of 'You can't even do this much for me! Do you know what so-and-so did for her?' and this would be supplemented by a long list of all the failures that he had had in his relationship with her so far.

At that moment, getting eaten by an alligator did not seem too bad in comparison. He sighed, clenched his beak in determination and dove down into the death traps, with the name of the *Vayu* God in his heart.

It was at his third attempt and after losing quite a few of his feathers that he was finally able to pluck the flower. More than once he had heard the unmistakable sound of the jaws of death snapping, and that small piece of land was littered with bones of half eaten birds. He was no nimble flyer himself, and it was only with luck and a sense of self-preservation that he arose after his third attempt and flew safely in the air.

The sun was already on its way to the west when he started his journey back, he couldn't fly too high because of the impeding darkness, all he remembered was the string of human villages that lay on the route, and he knew he could use their light as markers for going home. And as he flew back it was these thoughts that that enveloped his mind.

He had decided that this was the last time he would do something like this for her, and like the ten times before this he was trying to muster up courage and anger to stand up to her. He wanted to shout at her, tell her that either she was too stupid to keep on asking him to fulfil such tests of love, or he was basically an idiot who did not know what was good for him.

When he calmed down a bit he realized it was a bit of both. He then thought that he would rest his argument at the point that there must be at least a few months of gap between his adventures, because he knew (for reasons that he wasn't quite sure of) that there was no way that he could stop doing the things that he did for her.

After a while his mind completely eased and he entered that zone where he enjoyed flying. He was gliding happily for an hour even though the light had more or less been sucked away by the evening and distant star lights had decided that the time had come for them to make their presence felt. He even spotted a couple of his favourite fruit trees, and decided to go down and have a peck at them, but then decided against it because it would have meant keeping the flower down, leading to possible spoilage, and leading to definite anger/tantrum/sadness at home.

However, when hunger took over he relented and took a moments' rest on a tree when he was assured that his home was quite near to him. He gently kept the flower on a branch and looked around the tree for small berries which might be sampled.

'It's no use you know...' he heard a familiar voice croak from one of the trees behind him. It was the old parrot who lived on the same hill as him, the one with a habit of talking too much in different languages. He tried to hide his prejudice for the stupidity that comes in birds with old age and went up to him, 'Elder one, what is of no use?'

'It's no use your going home...our home is gone. It has flown away.'

He chuckled at the old parrot's habit of talking in riddles; still it felt good to talk to someone after a day where he had only alligators to talk to. He probed further, 'So our hill has flown away?'

'There was a monkey, you know...and he was big at one time, then small at another. And you know what he did...he came here big, and then became small, he went up our hill and jumped hither and thither as if searching for something.'

He listened to the incredulity of the whole thing, not knowing where this tale of the size changing monkey was heading.

'And then...the monkey, he became big again. He stepped away from the hill, and tore into the earth after folding his hands together like the humans do in their structures with bells inside.'

He was convinced that the parrot was making this story up because of his penchant of eating those leaves with the weird smell.

'And then...the monkey, he flew away, carrying the hill on one hand.'

He laughed, knowing that it was the effect of those leaves, these leaves made the parrot have 'high level' ideas about the future in which humans would destroy whole forests and how soon many birds would die altogether. Today these leaves had made him think of some giant/small monkey who had the ability of uprooting hills and flying away with them.

'Elder one when you feel normal again we will have another chat.' He laughed lightly and picked up the flower in his beak, he heard the very audible sigh of the parrot and paid no heed to it. Soon he was on his way home again.

Even in the dark he could figure out that something was definitely wrong. The horizon looked damaged. He looked down at the ground to see a circle of different animals standing around looking bewildered, and the birds in the trees knew that it was way beyond their natural waking time, and yet they chirped with the intensity of early morning calls.

And it didn't take him long to realize what was the reason for this odd behaviour of animals and birds. Something was suddenly missing from their forest, something that was home to all these animals and to him, and perhaps to all the birds crying agitated in the surroundings.

That something was a hill.

Somehow, between the time in the morning when he had left to get that flower and the time when night fell, the hill had disappeared. It looked as if it had been uprooted, because where the hill stood there was a rough uneven patch of earth.

He screamed in surprise as the flower fell from his mouth and twirled to the centre of rough patch below. He forgot his fatigue and started flying recklessly in all directions calling out her name. He knew (and hoped) that she would be in a tree somewhere here. He checked every bird he saw and asked every one he knew (including a few four-legged grass eaters, although his mother had often told him not to trust anyone or anything that moved around on four legs), but most of them were too dazed or too stupid to tell him where she was or what had happened.

He flew high in the air, whirled around in circles and kept on shouting her name trying in desperation to raise his voice above the din, he was hoping that she would somehow see him and signal to him. However, soon his body lost strength, and he glided downwards slowly.

'I told you...you know...flying monkey, flying hill.' The parrot had followed him to the tree near where their hill once stood. 'Now...there is nothing here. We must wait for the hill to either grow back or come back.'

'Elder one, I know she must have gone somewhere near. I know she will be back.' He spoke to the parrot, in an effort to give strength to himself.

'Who? What? The Hill? No I don't think our hill is near, we could have seen it otherwise you know.'

He sighed and took flight again, this time flying slowly and measuring the other flocks to see if anyone else was missing. All the other families seemed too dumbfounded and huddled together, because what had happened to their home was beyond comprehension. After flying for a while he came back to the tree where the parrot was sitting. The parrot had his favourite bunch of leaves in his beak, he kept it down and said, 'Here, eat a leaf, your mind will cool down, you will be able to think better.'

He sat in silence while the parrot munched on his leaves noisily; he tried to collect his thoughts. He knew that somehow the impossible had happened---a whole hill had disappeared.

And he was by now sure that she was still on the hill as it flew away, perhaps still asleep, or perhaps too scared to fly away. Absentmindedly he had started eating a leaf which the parrot had slyly pushed towards him.

As the juices from the leaf entered his body weird ideas started taking shape into his head. He was pretty sure that monkeys couldn't fly, and even if they had somehow learnt how to fly they would be no match for a bird as fast as him. He was also sure that someone carrying the weight of the hill would not be able to travel very fast.

Besides, he was a champion flier. He was not going to be out-flown by some monkey who had (either knowingly or unknowingly) kidnapped her. Monkeys are not supposed to be natural fliers. And he was sure of another thing---this leaf was giving him some very interesting thoughts, and he could now clearly comprehend the parrot's affinity for it.

'Elder one' he said, and he heard his voice as if it was an echo, 'I am going after her!'

'Hmmm...After whom? After the hill?'

'Yes. The hill and the monkey, and her!'

He flew straight up in the air with the bunch of leaves in his mouth, spurred on by the romantic notions of adventure and revenge. He was certain that before the sun rose again he would be with her. He knew that soon he would be confronting this monkey head-on, and that he currently had the anger in him that would make the monkey become all apologetic, and might change his manners too. After all, it is highly improper to steal someone's home and run away.

After a while he came down, realizing that he was forgetting something very important.

'Elder one...'

'Hmmm?'

'Which way did the monkey go?'

The parrot lazily pointed towards the south and went to a comfortable slumber.

He looked at the direction pointed out by the parrot and saw another adventure. He chirped happily, and found out that he could not stop chirping, his mind now had focus on only one thing---the distance that lay between her and him, and the eleventh adventure that she was about to put him through.

To complete the romanticism of it all he swooped down and picked the flower again, and then with the utmost speed that he could manage, he flew directly into the great wide open.

When she woke up she had a weird sensation that she had been flying in her sleep. And presently when she was awake, she observed that there were clouds around her, flying past at a great speed. She thought she was having a dream within a dream, and that she would need to sleep some more to escape this sensation.

She closed her eyes, and she slipped away.

A giant monkey would not have been able to go a long distance without resting for some time in between, he reasoned, and thus he started looking at the ground along the way for clues (like a giant footprint, or a hill-print) that would help him see if he was going in the right direction. He did not know whether it was the leaves that were stretching time or whether he had really been flying for a long time, but after what seemed like a day he saw the first sign that he was on the right path.

In a natural clearing next to a river there were clear signs that something humongous had been kept on the sandy bank and then picked up later. He flew down lower and saw a strange sight, there was a man holding a couple of those wooden things that humans wear on their foot, however, this man already had a pair of wooden things attached to his foot. He slowed his flight, and wished that he could speak human tongue, because this man (and the large crowd that was with him) would certainly have detained the monkey mid-flight, and would have an idea of why he was taking away that hill with him.

It was a loud noise of cheering that woke her up finally. She was annoyed, she liked to sleep and wake up at will (and the jungle where she stayed had a gentle noise rhythm that her body had already adjusted to) and this new form of noise was unacceptable. She looked around to make her discomfort felt to her lover, and found that he wasn't in eyesight. She cursed him, thinking he was perhaps off somewhere already with his friends, taking advantage of her being asleep.

She flew out of her tree to search for him, she glided along lazily around the hill, hoping to catch sight of him while thinking of things that she would tell him when he would come in her grasp, because slowly as sleep left her, she remembered that she had asked for a flower. And he had most probably failed in bringing her that flower (or had been too lazy to get it for her), because when she woke up, it wasn't to an image of him standing in front of her with the flower in his beak.

She puffed up full of anger and disappointment. She would punish him by not handing out any romantic tasks, she would make his life boring so that he would finally see how much she loved him. The anger in her kept her blind for some time to the fact that she was the only creature in the hill.

And that the hill was nowhere near the place that it usually was.

She flew high in the sky and looked down to see a very unfamiliar scene below her. Her home was surrounded by many hills, and she presently stared at one small hill standing in a dusty clearing with few and no trees around it.

Anger quickly gave way to fear as she realized that something was seriously amiss. Her neighbours, her friends, her lover, everyone had disappeared. And she too had magically come to this weird place which looked nothing like her home. She quickly spiralled down to the ground, trying to maintain her control. She needed to stabilize and think of what had happened. She needed to take a deep breath and relax. Perhaps this was a dream, perhaps she needed to go to sleep once more to wake up back to a reality where her lover would be standing next to her and her home would be in its right place.

He had lost track of the distance that he had covered, one thing was sure that the monkey had only stopped at one place in his flight, and had flown quickly to a great distance, because in the changing landscape below him (which now looked like a huge field full of hills and mountains cut in half) contained no signs of giant monkey footprints. He had stopped in a forest near a human settlement and talked to a couple of owls (the few birds who do stay awake in the night), they confirmed that the general direction that he was heading in was right, and they had seen a flying mountain with a huge monkey attached to it, but he was going at a great speed, and thus they would not be able to give a detailed description.

They also told him that sadly a small bird like him can never hope to match pace with the monkey, who was moving as if he was born of the god of wind himself. The bird took offense to this. He said, '*Vayu Dev* is the God of birds too, I do not believe that any son of his would harm us! You are mistaken, and here in front of you I swear by the God of wind that I shall fly with utmost force aided by His agents, and that I shall rescue her from the flying hill and bring her back!'

The owls did not mind his irate soliloquy. They knew a hopeless romantic when they saw one. They were great supporters of romance themselves, and they told the bird that the owls had in fact become such nocturnal birds because of the fact that many generations ago they had been a race of romantics who were used to staying up in the night, pining for the love of their lives.

The owls also did not mind when the bird flew away while they were in the middle of their exposition. All owls are born old, and their rationale was that his haste as being one of the follies of youth.

While he flew across an entire subcontinent, she sat at the frayed edge of a battle that raged between bipeds and quadrupeds. The bipeds were bigger than those that she was used to seeing, and more ferocious. And the quadrupeds were led by two bipeds; one of them had skin as black as the reflection of a moonless night in the pond. The quadrupeds were monkeys and bears. And they matched the ferocity of the bipeds that they fought against.

The war sounds and mayhem unsettled her, but whenever she caught a glimpse of the black biped she always felt a calm run through her. Besides, the monkeys and bears had a giant monkey fighting for them; there was no way that they were going to be defeated. After her first day in the war zone she mustered courage in the evening to go near the black biped. She knew that he was at the centre of this war and thus he would somehow know the reasons for why and how she had been transported here.

The bipeds spoke at ease with the monkeys and the bears, conversing in a common language which did not match with any sound of the jungle. She waited till they finished their conference and then took the risk of slowly alighting on the shoulder of the black one. It seemed he didn't mind her polite intrusion in his privacy, he continued talking to the other biped paying no particular heed to her.

Then softly he raised his hand and put his palm in front of her in form of an invitation. She stepped on to the palm gingerly at first, but once she came into complete contact of his hand she felt the comfort of sleeping in semi-soft dead leaves. The black biped used three fingers to gently caress her back, and after the third or fourth stroke she felt herself heavy with sleep again.

She closed her eyes and she slipped away.

She had been used to clean dreamless sleep, but this particular time she saw that she was having a very vivid dream. It seemed that she was standing in some sort of hall all alone until in front of her a black bird materialized slowly. And it was quite a peculiar thing that this black bird resembled the biped on whose palm she had fallen asleep.

'I have taken this form my child to communicate with you.' His voice was deep and yet bird-like. 'When you sat on my shoulder and tried to speak in my ear something told me that inadvertently I have caused you great pain. You are afraid, is it the war that troubles you? Do not worry; it will get over in a day or two. And then this entire land will once again know lasting peace.'

She looked at him blankly, and then found her voice, 'Kind sir, the war is the least of my worries. I don't know where I am and I don't know how I got here. The last thing that I remember is sleeping peacefully, as I assume I am sleeping now. But then I woke up to see that my home was not where my home used to be, and my betrothed isn't around to comfort me.'

The black bird regarded her with gentle eyes, his vision piercing her and reading her past, present and future in the same instance. Then the bird smiled and said, 'The *Pawan Putr* had taken utmost care of not harming a single creature when he brought the hill here. But he had perhaps not accounted for a particularly sound sleeper. My child I apologize on my friends behalf, in the urgency to save my brother's life he made this mistake. I pray you forgive him.'

The bird bowed down her head and said 'Kind sir, you mentioned that it was the son of the God of winds who brought me here. This really does have some divine significance then, and I don't know who you are sir but if you have the son of *Pawan* helping you in the battle then perhaps your brother's life must be really important.'

The black bird chuckled and said 'All lives are important dear child. Now, we know how you came here, do you wish for us to find a way to send you back?'

'Not yet sir, allow me, in whatever way I can to be able to help you in this war. And in the meantime I am sure that my betrothed is already on his way to take me back, after all I am not *very* far from home, am I?'

The black bird smiled, 'Bless you my child. It is but a matter of days before all this would be over.'

He did not know how long he had flown, he knew that days and nights had passed and that he should have been feeling very very tired. Instead he felt hunger and a single-minded motivation to go on. He had crossed many different types of hills and mountains and serpentine rivers flowing through forests taking a path as straight as he could (although at times he shuddered thinking what if the flying monkey had strayed from this line). On one of those days of continuous flight he saw that the greenery below was fast disappearing and on the horizon was a vast expanse of blue water.

He looked down to see where the land was about to end and decided that it was time for him to take rest. Unfortunately, the remains of a giant bird caught his eye and he knew that this was a decidedly bad omen.

He spiralled down in a hurry and he sat next to the remaining bones of the gigantic bird. He knew he was staring at what might have once been a mighty warrior, a king among birds, perhaps a direct agent of *Vayu Dev*. And in that moment he started crying slowly, he looked at the bones and then at the water that covered three horizons in front of him. He felt dizzy and inadequate, he somehow felt that his entire quest had been futile and that there was only one thing left for him to do. He would try and fly across this huge sheet of water, he would succeed or he would die trying.

Being parched he decided that he would start his remaining journey after taking a sip of water, he tasted a drop and immediately spat it out.

This water was like nothing he had ever tasted before. But he was thirsty and he knew that drinking water was necessary. He tried to take another sip but his body rejected it once again. He looked around to see if there was any other source of water. He saw an old bear sitting on the grainy surface leaning against a smooth rock. The bear had a bowl lying in front of him, the bird took his chances and flew near the bear, delighted to see that the bowl contained water. He cautiously took a sip and rejoiced to find that it was sweet water which he was used to drinking.

He drank his fill, sang happily, pecked lightly at the feet of the sleeping bear in gratitude and prepared to conquer water.

The next thing to do was to follow a path of stones which lead straight into the water, this he did to measure the straightness of his direction, he knew that otherwise with three horizons looking exactly the same it would be very hard for him to find the right way.

He had thought that flying across water would be relaxing since the area near rivers and lakes in his home had always been cool. However the first resistance which he faced was in form of the strong wind which kept pushing him back towards the grainy surface. It took a lot of effort for him to break that wind barrier when he was suddenly faced with the opposite problem. Now the wind pushed him from behind and made it impossible for him to control his flight. With a prayer to the *Vayu Dev* on his lips he tried to steady himself and follow the path of the rocks but the gusts of wind lead him astray.

Once he found a semblance of control in his flying, he was finally able to soak in the view that this part of the journey afforded him. The sheet of water below him teamed with uncountable fishes, some of them as large as the gigantic bird he had seen on the shore, others which seemed quite small but swam together so as to look like a large fish.

He also saw a large serpentine creature swimming around lazily in the water, this creature was given a wide berth by the others. And it was perhaps the light of the sun playing tricks on his eyes with the reflection on water but it seemed that this creature looked up, spotted the bird and smiled, looking both dangerous and beautiful at the same time.

The bird saw other birds too flying above the ocean, some of them forming a shape that looked like a giant bird, and in this they mimicked the fish in the oceans below. But after some time he saw that he was the only bird in that patch of sky, the fish in the ocean below continuously seemed to be bigger. It was that part of the day when the sun's light was the harshest, and somehow it had the effect of reflecting upon him from time to time from the ocean's surface. This temporarily blinded him.

Perhaps it was the heavy water laden wind and the direct sunlight above him but soon the bird started finding it difficult to remain conscious. There were a couple of times when he found that he had fallen asleep gliding across the wind and it was when he had started rapidly losing height the pull from below had woke him up.

The third time he almost dozed off he gave up, he knew he had come this far and he knew that somehow ending this journey would make him meet his lover, but now it seemed that all his strength left him. He let the *Vayu Dev* take him away, knowing that he was half-dead because he had started seeing visions.

After-all how else could he explain that at a far distance ahead of him he could see the flying monkey coming towards him accompanied by a flying house, one of those small houses that the bipeds attached to chariots, and in his entire life and all that he had heard about bipeds he knew that such houses could not fly.

With the name of the *Vayu Dev* on his beak he embraced his fate and started falling freely towards the ocean.

Only to be caught in a furry palm. He did not know whether he was dead or alive, but he remembered looking at the giant monkey who had caught him and saying 'Thief...' before he dozed off.

It was a very strange reunion for the lovers, they had been separated by the flying monkey and now had been reunited on this flying chariot. There were bipeds present, but they paid little heed to the two birds except for smiling occasionally in their direction and giving them small pieces of grain along with bowls of sweet flavoured water. His lover kept gushing incessantly with the story that she had to tell and it took at least three of her incoherent rambling sessions for him to grasp fully that she had been witness to a great story (he did not mind at that time telling her that he had in the meantime scripted a story of his own), he chuckled and smiled with her, ignoring the full weight of the physical and mental exhaustion that his journey had wrought over him. He also agreed to listen to her story for a fourth time on a very simple condition: she would never ever send him to another adventure.

MR MARKETING MANAGER

There was certain flamboyance about him. Most of which was make-believe, a facade which he carried with himself, a swagger with which he strutted around. The reason for this was that he lived a dual life, and it was imperative for him to stay in character, both in office and outside it.

But I am getting ahead of myself, it is important to properly introduce the main character of this story. Let us start with his name: Kumar Johnson. His name was an amalgamation of the two cultures which he belonged to, a *Mumbaiya* Catholic boy who was part of a mixed family of Konkani Goans and Christians. He was of the variety who wore an open check-shirt over a T-shirt and got away with it because of our office's rather casual dress code. A wrist band in his left hand and a shiny watch on his right (because we were in the business of selling watches, his wearing a gaudy watch of our own company was rather excusable). And he had a rather relaxed job, no pressure of sales, numbers, month ends, etc. You see he was not in the Sales team, Kumar Johnson was our company's 'Marketing Officer'.

A Marketing Officer can be responsible for a lot of things, making sure that our brand is visible throughout the region, capturing data to see how branding and marketing activities helps in sales, or performing BTL to aid in sales. But what Kumar did was mostly putting up visuals of our products at our dealer points whenever he got a budget from the corporate office on his whims so that he could make a PowerPoint presentation and send it to the brand team and earn some brownie points. On many occasions he did this without the dealer's consent or requirement or informing the sales officer, leading to a lot of friction between the sales team and the dealers. However, that entire aspect of him can be a different story all together.

You see this story is not about what Kumar Johnson did in his work, it is about what he believed that he did. And this is where the facade comes into the picture.

This whole thing began on a Monday morning. I was sitting on my chair in my cubicle grappling with dealer-offtake data and trying to make sense of how this month's targets could be broken down into them. I had taken a printout of the data and was looking at it with utmost concentration when I heard a dull thud, and presently I looked up to see that Kumar Johnson had dropped a pile of cards on my desk. He dragged a chair from the next cubicle not bothering to see whether its occupant was about to return to it any time soon. He had a mad grin on his face, the kind that made me want to knock him over with a single punch (and in the process removing a few teeth).

'Look! Look, no?' He said eagerly.

I looked. The cards were visiting cards, and they did not match in any way with the white regulation cards that were issued to us with our designation and the company logo embossed on top. These cards were bright yellow in colour and they had a black border, the logo of the company was relegated to a corner. The cards proudly pronounced

Mr Kumar Johnson

Marketing Head

His grin became bigger, 'Solid! Isn't it?'

I sighed, 'Mr Kumar Johnson,' I said, 'Are you not a Marketing Officer and not the *Marketing Head* of the company?'

'Correct!' Kumar said loudly, and then suddenly lowered his voice conspiratorially, 'But this is something that you know, and I know, and people linked to our company know. But not the outside world, no?'

'No.' I said, already regretting being part of this conversation.

'To the world outside...' he said with as much dramatic flourish he could manage in a whisper, 'I am Kumar Johnson, the head of marketing of India's biggest watch brand.'

'Is this what you are going around telling everyone? Are you out of your mind?'

He looked shocked, 'Tchah! What? No of course not! Not everyone...'

'Good because you could get into...'

'Only the hot *mulghi log* that I fancy, then what?'

A ridiculous scheme to attract women, tell them you are a hot-shot marketing head of a big company, and if the girl is gullible enough and if you have Kumar Johnson's chutzpah then it was quite plausible that he would be able to get someone with the help of this fake personality.

And of course Mumbai with its immense sea of humanity has no shortage of the gullible. They are all out there somewhere in this city. And Kumar Johnson was a master of finding out this somewhere. He had a master's degree in finding out girls and dating them for a short period. He relied heavily on props like above, not telling anyone that he was a lowly paid and placed employee in his company, and that is where his make-believe swagger and flamboyance came into the picture.

It would have become obvious to you, dear reader, that I do not look kindly upon Kumar Johnson. I dislike people who are fake, and I also disliked his general attitude towards women and how he dumped them frequently, usually after getting them to have sex with him. And yet I could not get rid of him or stay away from him because Kumar was in a strange way unavoidable.

Both of us lived in Thane and more often than not even though I did not will it to happen we travelled together to work. If I caught the 8:27 CST Fast, I would see him grinning in the same coach hanging for dear life just outside the door, and if I took the Income Tax Bus in the morning he would be at the bus stand waving animatedly at me. And God forbid if he got a seat next to me, the chap would keep on talking until we reached Sion, not stopping for a second and robbing me of precious thirty minutes of sleep.

Thus, throughout his career at our company he chose to inflict himself upon me, and after a certain point of time he started considering me as a close friend and confidante. I, being a nice sort of guy, never told him to get lost and instead endured him with patience.

It was after a couple of weeks post his hair-brained card printing scheme that he caught me on the bus and jostled the people around us to get a seat next to me. He was literally beaming as if he had brushed with an extra dose of Colgate today.

'Guess what?'

'What?' I said lazily, not really wanting to talk to him.

'Guess, no?'

'Seriously, what?'

'Tchah! You are no fun. See this!' He produced his fake card in front of me.

'Kumar', I said, 'I have already seen this card of yours, and if you would be so kind as to let me sleep I would actually treat you to a full chicken meal at *Varde's'*

'Wait re!' He said, and then like a clumsy magician he rubbed his forefinger and thumb and thus produced another card from beneath. It was a simple white card with a blue typeface on it, it said

Himani Kelkar

Product Manager, HUL

I snatched that card from his hand and said, 'You have started to impersonate girls also?'

He snatched the card back. 'Heh! You totally underestimate me Bhau, *arre* this is the girl I netted no? Over the weekend only!'

I looked at him in disbelief, 'Are you serious? You are dating some hot-shot Product Manager from HUL?'

'Solid, isn't it?'

I mulled over this, 'Must be quite old?'

'Tchah! *Nako baba,* she's a total *chhabbis. Mast mirchi maal.* She is from one of those good colleges, IIM-ShaiM, one of those. And total *pataoed* her I have.'

I stayed silent for a while, then I spoke, 'And she thinks that you are the Marketing Head, no less, of our company?'

'Then what!'

'And...You expect me to believe this.'

He laughed, not caring for the fact that he disturbed a whole bunch of thirty-minute sleepers in the bus, 'Not at all! That is why I want you to take a look at this!' And he showed me a Polaroid photograph of his standing with a girl in front of the Gateway of India.

The girl was homely, but she had a very pretty smile, and inwardly I felt sorry for her for landing with such a creep like Kumar. 'How do I know that this is not one of your old girlfriends?'

He laughed again, 'Hard man to please you are, *arre* she is the real deal. I am telling you no, life is set for me for the next few months.' And then he closed his eyes and leaned back, perhaps envisioning what the next few months would be like.

I shook him out of his reverie, 'She is not one of your regular run of the mill girls now, is she?'

'No baba, not at all.'

'Where exactly did you meet her?'

'Oh, somewhere re.'

Again with his somewhere, 'Nevermind, look Kumar, as a colleague I must warn you that this girl will expect a certain lifestyle from you. She is from a good company and a good college herself and she knows what being the marketing head of a company means. How are you going to manage?'

He turned towards me suddenly, 'Glad that you asked, see since this is only a matter of a few months can you lend me some money?'

It was my turn to close my eyes and lean back, I muttered an audible 'Go to hell'.

Over the next month or so he continued to intermittently tell me how good his relationship with Himani was going. I asked him once whether he intended to tell her the truth, and he brushed it off again saying that it was only a matter of few months. I waited patiently to see whether he would fall flat on his face or actually get away with it. Past experience told me that it was more plausible that the latter would happen.

And then one fine day he came to me with a big frown on his face, 'We need to talk. Also, I need to smoke.'

The urgency in his tone and the twelve o'clock on his face made me hurry down to the cigarette shop with him, he bought a Gold Flake and started puffing furiously, and he walked away nonchalantly from the cigarette shop fully expecting me to pay for the cigarette. I asked him, 'When did you start smoking?'

He said, 'When there is too much tension then only I smoke. Very occasional. And my friend, the time has come with too much tension.'

I chided him, 'What tension? You are not in sales! You have no month-ends, where is the tension? Where is the pressure?'

'She got pregnant.' He blurted out, along with mouthfuls of cigarette smoke.

For a few seconds I was shocked, and then just to make sure that both of us were on the same track, I asked him 'You mean the HUL girl don't you? You got her pregnant?'

'Yes Bhau! I...I really don't know how it happened!'

'With your kind of experience I thought you would already know how these things work.'

'Baba, serious matter. I took all precaution, I don't know how it happened, but...yesterday evening she comes and tells me.'

I waited for a while and then said, 'So....Congratulations?'

'Tchah! No time for *masti* this Bhau. I never intended for this to happen...'

'Obviously.'

'Listen Bhau I really need a very big favour.'

'If it is money you can forget it. I don't have any, and even if I did I wouldn't really give any away to...'

'No! Bhau you read me wrong! Total different favour this. Only you can help me.'

I contemplated the choice of my next few words, by that time he had finished off his cigarette, crushed it roughly on the ground and had helped himself to another one. 'Okay, I am listening to you. If it is not related to money I might be willing to help. But please stress on the word *might*.'

He closed in again, blowing smoke almost exactly inside my ears, 'This is all to be very hush-hush.'

'Go on.'

'You remember you told me about the Doctor brother-in-law of yours?'

I could see where this was headed, and yet I urged him to continue.

'You remember? The one with the big clinic-shlinic in Mulund.'

'I remember him quite well Kumar, after all he does happen to be my brother-in-law by chance.'

'Yes, same guy! Listen,' Now he was almost chewing at my ears, 'Can he...can he help me with an abortion.'

'No.' I told him firmly, 'He most decidedly cannot. And even if he could I wouldn't tell him to. What you are doing is wrong.'

'But why? Why will you not tell him? And why can't he help me with the abortion?'

'Well for starters, because he is a dentist.'

I saw some sort of hope in his eyes getting dim as the cigarette on his lips fell down on the ground and I left him there to pay for the second cigarette himself.

The Gods of chance and happenstance were kind on me for the next one month or so since I barely saw Kumar again during that period, however, on one particular Saturday (when the trains from Thane towards Kurla are relatively emptier)

I saw him occupying a window seat. He had a terribly morose look on his face, and I genuinely felt sorry for him. This is one of the perils of being someone who is nice in general. I went up and squeezed myself next to him.

'You look sad. What happened, did you get the abortion?'

He shook his head in the negative.

'Happy Father's Day.' I said and put out my hand for a handshake. He glared at me and I chuckled, imitating him, 'Come on Johnson Bhau, take a joke, no?'

But then I saw that he was almost on the verge of crying and stopped. 'Okay, no more jokes. Sorry, tell me what happened.'

In between stifled sobs he told me, 'I am about to get married.'

'To the HUL girl? I am proud of you Kumar! You are doing the right thing!' I honestly did not believe that this was the same Kumar that I knew, 'But why are you crying?'

'It...is because...I am forced to marry her, her brother's friend's father...or something...bloody MLA from Thane.'

This was a twist in the tale, 'What?'

'They...they will break all bones in my body...and cut off important stuff if I don't.'

Part of me said that it served him right, but then part of me also wished to console him. He produced a wedding invitation card from his bag and said in a very shaky voice, 'Do come. But don't tell a lot of people in the company about this...it's...a matter of some shame.'

The wedding date was about a week from the day he gave me the card, this looked like a very rushed job. I sat quietly thinking of things that I could tell him to make it better, and then I struck upon the most obvious one.

'Look Kumar, don't take it the wrong way, but consider this. Even that girl is sort of getting forced to marry you. And all things said and done, you are actually getting married ...she must be earning loads and...of course you will have to tell her the truth that...'

At the mention of 'earning loads' he literally started bawling.

'Shh...' I said, 'Calm down Kumar! People are looking, come on why do you have to cry...it isn't all bad.'

In between fits of hysterical sobbing he said, 'I am crying because...because the bitch lied to me!'

'Lied to you, how? Is she not pregnant?'

'No! Not about that! She isn't some Product Manager in HUL, she isn't even on HUL payroll! She is just a data entry operator for an HUL distributor. Her visiting card was fake!'

That day for the entire journey from Thane to Kurla Johnson kept on crying like a mad man and I kept on laughing like crazy until tears started coming out of my eyes.

MEETING JD SIR

I have spent a fourth of my current life span in the city of Baroda and it has grown on me. It has enveloped me by giving me memories and moments for a long haul. Of the total of seven years that I have lived there, I went away for seven more after year five and came back to the city older, though definitely not wiser.

I had finished college as an Engineer and the only job that I had netted had given me a joining date which gave me a year at home twiddling my thumbs. I did what everyone in this country does, post finishing Engineering, and started preparing for MBA entrance exams.

The fact that I had to carry this out in the city of Baroda was agreeable to me, I had spent the more enjoyable years of my childhood here, and the small-bigness of the city was endearing. Even if you lived in the farthest corner of the city, you were still never too far away from anyone or anything.

And over the years the basic things had remained the same, except for a few necessary but ugly flyovers that had sprouted across the city, like the roads had decided to take an *angdai* and then froze in the act, the restaurants, the halls, malls, everything was more or less how I had left it in 2002.

However, there was one change, in my second stint in Baroda---I had fewer friends. Most of my school friends had left the city, and I had the sensation of someone who had come to a party to find out that it was already late and people have left and it was now up to him to switch off the lights and shut the gate.

But a few old friends still remained in the city, some of them who were firmly rooted there and had no intention of moving because they had to look after their family businesses or had worked there, and there were others who had studied in and around Baroda, and were, like me, between jobs or deciding colleges.

I had intermittently been in touch with my friends post coming back to Baroda, meeting them up when they floated in and out of the city and in and out of my life, and it was one of these friends who called me on a pleasantly cool December evening and told me that JD sir was in town and it was possible for me to go and meet him.

JD sir was our maths teacher in school, he kept his concepts and classes simple, taught efficiently and more often than not side-stepped traditionally solved examples. He used around 40 to 50% of the total time allotted to him to finish the syllabus and it was what he did in the rest of the time that made him memorable.

JD sir was a good raconteur; he loved to talk and to tell stories. Through telling of his tales he became the most personal of all our teachers, and for some in the class he was the closest teacher that they had. He was in turns strict, jocular, enigmatic and humble. He had had suffered a lot of hardships in Bombay where he lived earlier, and he often told us about them, but he painted his struggle in a positive light, trying to fit in an inspirational anecdote whenever he could. He had a good sense of humour, and if a class adjacent to you was erupting in laughter at odd intervals the chances of it being JD sir's session were quite high. Getting close is a two-way street, the more he opened up to the class on a regular basis, the more people found it easy to open up to him. For many of us he was the go-to teacher for any kind of problems in school. JD sir was considered cool. He was sorted, and because he was sorted it was easy for him to help you out as well.

And therein also lay a problem, he made it a point to know as much as possible about his students as a result of which there were times when he would also start interfering in the school lives of his students. If he condoned of two students being friends, he made his displeasure public. The seating arrangement for his class had to be different than that of other teachers. And his humour would at times be targeted towards a particular student, laced heavily with sarcasm he would roast any student on a good or bad day. In some ways there were positives to his closeness to his students because he got a chance to counsel students in trouble, motivate them for exams and allow them to let some steam off in the pressure cooker that our country's educational system is. And that is why among all our teachers JD sir would perhaps get the highest rating in both love and hate, if I took a survey of my schoolmates two years junior and senior it would be quite possible that JD sir would the one most remembered.

For me it was neither love nor hate. I found JD sir immensely interesting because of the way opinion about him was divided in the class. In my own circle of friends I had one who was absolutely devoted to JD sir to the point that he went to him for advice on how to get close to the girl in class that he had a crush on (JD sir told him to concentrate on studies and not in this relationship nonsense, but also ended up giving him a tip to use) and one who could not stand his face or even the letters J and D in the English alphabet. Personally I had very few run-ins with him, he mostly let me be, picking on me only when he wanted someone to sing in class, and it was something that I positively looked forward to since I enjoyed inflicting the population around me with my singing voice. Like me he was a big fan of Jackie Chan, especially of his earlier work like Project A, Police Story and Drunken Master. And he was fairly unbiased when it came to doling out marks in the term exams. But we were never close.

JD sir left the school around the same time that I did, while I left the school because I had to leave Baroda altogether he left it to pursue entrepreneurial ambitions. New Era had come up with guidelines which meant that any teacher who taught in the school could not have private tuition coaching classes in the evening, the basic intention behind this being noble perhaps because teachers have a chance of unduly forcing students to join their evening coaching classes. However, most teachers undertook separate coaching classes because it gave them a chance to supplement their income, and the Indian education system does not really pay well unless you are a teacher in the most famous school of the city, and sometimes not even then.

Without really piling his financial troubles on us JD sir often told us how difficult it was to cope up with rising expenses on a salary that hardly brought him inside the tax bracket. So it was no surprise when after completing the 2001--02 school year JD sir resigned and set up a small coaching centre consisting of a single classroom in an area near the school which had other coaching classes as well. Even less surprising was that many of my classmates joined. Here, he was free to decide his salary by the number of students that he taught, and could continue what he loved doing best with most of his favourite students.

After leaving Baroda the phone calls that made to the city were centred more on how my friends were faring, and how the girl I had a crush on was faring or whether there were any new pretty girls in the school or in my friends' lives. Teachers tend to get missed out.

And thus it was some time after the actual event that in the course of a conversation involving 'who is where now' I got to know from a friend that JD sir had left the country, he had gone to New Zealand to become a teacher there and I remember thinking at the time when I got the news that it was good for him since New Zealand would decidedly pay more than Baroda.

Now, seven years and seven months after I had originally left Baroda and five and a half years after JD sir had left for New Zealand, I got a call from Ravi (one of the rooted Barodians, he was studying Medicine, and when you study Medicine you stay a student for ten years or so) who told me that JD sir was in the city for a few days and would be available to meet during evenings. In my year of doing nothing it was easy for me to quickly decide that I did want to meet JD sir. I asked Ravi if he would accompany me but he refused saying he had already met sir once and was about to go out of town, and it was while he was going out of town that he somehow remembered that he should inform me about JD sir.

He had given me a landline number on which to call up and confirm the time since unlike me JD sir had a paucity of time (later I would come to know that it was in fact the first time that he had come back to India and had to meet a lot of people as well as take care of a lot of work). When I called up that number I encountered his wife, Ranjana ma'am, who taught primary classes at our school. I had thought there would be a dim chance that JD sir would remember who I was, Ranjana ma'am would hardly know me, and yet she perhaps filed me under ex-students of JD sir' and told me to come at five thirty in the evening.

It was when I actually took an auto towards my destination that I realized that coupled with the chance of JD sir not recognizing me or mistaking me for someone else was the fact that I really would not know what to talk about with him. But perhaps it was also a trip that I was taking for myself. A door that opened to a part of my childhood that I cherished a lot, which I had come across when the universe conspired to throw me back in Baroda. If for nothing else it would be two people who left this city for a long period of time and could always use a little reminiscing. And I also looked forward to JD sir recollecting school stories from the time that I was actually in school and telling them in his signature style.

From an old and faithful video library along the way I bought a DVD of the Police Story trilogy hoping JD sir retained his love for Jackie Chan.

It was a row house located next to the school where I had studied, I stopped the auto a fair distance from my destination because I wanted to walk next to the bricked building where Christmas decorations were getting swept away from the ground by faces I did not recognize. After coming back to Baroda I had yet to visit the school because if one thing had changed it was the school's security rules, it was no longer possible for an ex-student to waltz inside without prior business.

When I reached the exact address a fat and lazy dog greeted me on the door, it was a huge dog with golden fur who regarded me with a half-hearted sniff and then lay its head back on the floor. Having a near mortal fear of big fat dogs, I decided to stay as far away as possible until someone would usher me in.

It was Ranjana ma'am who came to the door and told me to come in and not be afraid (or words to that effect) since the dog did not bite anyone at all and added something about him being rather ineffective as a guard dog. The house like a lot of Gujarati houses that I had been to, had a small ante-chamber which served as the drawing room and was the area made accessible to visitors, etc., in this room was a sofa set, a *diwan* and a small coffee table. JD sir was sitting with his legs crossed on the *diwan*, and as soon as I looked at him I remembered why Sanshit and I had given him the nick name 'Eskimo'.

Baroda doesn't really experience temperatures below 20 degrees even at the peak of winters. December in Baroda provides you an entire air-cooled city to walk in, and mostly a shirt with a half sweater suffices, but JD sir always wore three layers of clothing, he had a bomber jacket which was his trademark style. And living in New Zealand had not increased his immunity towards cold, he was still swathed in warm clothes wearing a different but similar looking bomber jacket and had stuffed his hands inside the pockets.

The second thing that struck me was how old he looked. JD sir always had a head full of grey hair, that had not changed much but his face was thinner, his face looked gaunt, but his eyes though still had the same sparkle which he had when he taught his classes. He looked at me and smiled 'Welcome Vaibhav. You look the same, Ranjana doesn't he still look the same?' I did not look the same, I had lost a lot of weight since the time that I was in school, and was currently halfway through gaining it all back.

I sat down awkwardly on the sofa and said, 'Sir...you also haven't changed at all.' I lied inefficiently. I handed over the Police Story DVD to him muttering something about Christmas, his smile became a pleasant chuckle and he placed the pack carefully on the coffee table 'Police Story has always been one series that I can watch again and again, although the third part wasn't that great.' He turned again towards Ranjana ma'am and said, 'Vaibhav was a very sincere student.' And at that moment I realized that I was correct in my suspicion, he didn't really remember me too well. I had never been even close to the definition of sincere. Or perhaps JD sir remembered me but was just being polite.

'Could you please get some tea for us?' He asked ma'am, she nodded and went inside. Then without preamble JD sir started speaking, 'This is the house of my friends. They have been taking care of Anmol ever since Ranjana moved to New Zealand.' As if on cue a portly gentleman of about fifty entered the room, shook my hand and took his place on the *diwan*. He did not find me out of place at his home, I wasn't the first student to have visited JD sir recently.

'So tell me Vaibhav, what are you doing in Baroda these days? Hadn't you moved away to someplace in UP?'

I mentioned that I was between college-and-job and was currently biding my time with MBA preparations.

'MBA? Good good. So, which college did you go to?'

When I mentioned that I had cleared the JEE and had studied at Banaras Hindu University his eyes brightened, 'I always knew you would crack JEE!' He said, 'See Ranjana, I told you he was very sincere! Which company did you land a job in?'

I sheepishly mentioned the low-paying software job that I had landed and he frowned, 'But isn't BHU a good...and weren't you...never mind.' To my relief he quickly changed the topic, 'Leave all that, tell me how come you are back in Baroda?'

I tried to be clever and made a remark about prodigal sons returning, he guffawed and said, 'That makes the two of us! Although unfortunately I am here only for a short time. But this city is special, aren't you happy that you are getting to spend some time here?'

Baroda is a subject on which I can talk at length, I smiled and told sir something that PG Wodehouse had said about New York, coming back to the city is like meeting an old sweetheart and finding that she had put on some weight. My feelings about Baroda were roughly the same.

JD sir was pleased with my comparison, he said, 'If things were better, and one day things might again be better I will perhaps come back and settle here. This city gave me a lot many kids, your batch,' he pointed a benevolent finger at me, 'your batch in particular has given me a lot of love.'

Then we rattled names back and forth to see how many both of us remembered, JD sir had once said in his class that he never forgot any of his students name and/or face and when it came to the class of 2004 his claim rang true more than 90% of the time. Call it the Roshomon effect but we had differing perceptions or opinions about many students and many classmates, 'Wasn't he the one who went to the states?' he would quip, 'Was he not the one with the very bad handwriting but a good brain?' We stopped at the mention of Sonam, she was perhaps the closest student to him and conversely Sonam too considered JD sir to be her favourite teacher. In the bubbling enthusiasm of the bonhomie that had started to surround us I blurted out that she was getting married.

'Is she now?' He stroked his chin, 'Yes, I remember someone...Ravi?...telling me about it. Or perhaps it was Sonam herself. Don't you think she is getting married too early? How old are you kids? Twenty three?'

I said that it was a love marriage, and since she had already found someone, had almost completed her master's degree and her prospective in-laws encouraged her working post marriage.

He smiled, not so much because of the explanation I gave but because of the way I said it, He told ma'am, 'See Ranjana how these kids have grown up. You never used to be this articulate in school.'

Ma'am had come back with a tray full with four cups of tea and a plate of butter biscuits. The tea stopped conversation for a while, it was strong and syrupy, I had forgotten to mention my preference for unsweetened tea but the ginger in the tea enhanced its taste. I resisted the urge to dip a biscuit into the cup and drink it, to restart conversation I broached the topic of New Zealand and how he managed to go there since we had almost run out of people and events to talk about. JD sir immediately grew sombre, 'I was surfing the net one day, I believe it was in the school library, and then suddenly there was this pop-up ad, it said 'Work in New Zealand' or 'Teach in New Zealand' or something and I immediately clicked on it. And then I filled up a form, and that is where this started.'

I was about to laugh waiting for the punch line because I believed that JD sir was telling this in his trademark dead-pan jocular style, and some intuition stopped me from doing so in the nick of the time. I could see that JD sir was dead serious. That he had actually done the opposite of what should be done with pop-up ads and had gone on to click on one. And then he had proceeded to follow what the pop-up ad told him to do.

I kept the shock out of my voice and asked with intrigue on whether it was some agency or the NZ government which had taken out the ad.

JD sir sighed trying to keep out the disappointment out of his voice, 'They overpromised Vaibhav. And they didn't quite deliver. I uprooted my life from here and went to their country, thinking that they genuinely needed teachers. All they wanted was temps.'

I asked him if he had temped for a couple of years and then found a permanent job.

'No', he said as he lazily cracked his fingers, 'For five and a half years all I have been doing in New Zealand are temp jobs.' He spoke emotionlessly, 'There have in fact been periods where there were no jobs at all. It was not what I thought it would be.'

I knew how the temp system worked, and how he would have found work only when a teacher from a school went on an extended period of leave. I tried to lighten his mood by telling him about one of my favourite movies in which a temp teacher forms a rock band out of the students that he is teaching, but seeing that his interest waned, I stopped.

There was another period of silence; I tried filling it by asking him where his son was.

'Anmol plays badminton for an hour every evening, he still likes it here. Like you, he too loves Baroda and doesn't like the idea of leaving it.'

After another spell of silence JD sir spoke, 'But not all things are bad, Ranjana joined me two years after I went to New Zealand and she has found a permanent job. She is doing quite well.'

I asked him how life in New Zealand was different from India.

'There are a lot of facilities in New Zealand, for example, if you want to get electricity fixed then all you need to do is to give a call to the local electrician and it will be done for free. But then it is not entirely free, they give you all these facilities but they really fleece you when it comes to taxes.'

I made a bad joke about a country used to fleecing because of the number of sheep there. I wanted to tell him that it was perhaps not worth living there, instead I asked him if he had plans on settling back in India.

The sparkle in JD sir's eyes returned and he said, 'I have not even begun to get settled there and you want me to come back to India. It has been only a few years there Vaibhav, my struggle in Bombay started when I was fifteen years old, and I made it in Bombay, I think I can make it in New Zealand. JD is not one to leave a place without leaving his mark! Why are you smiling?'

I was smiling because what he said reminded me of the song 'New York, New York.' I told him that Bombay is like

New York, if you can make it there, you will make it anywhere. This made him smile too. I made a promise to email him an mp3 version of the song (although I forgot to note his email address).

His mood was less sombre now, and I could see him looking at and working towards building himself a good life in New Zealand. We talked some more about New Zealand, I tried staying on the positive aspects of the life there, the weather, the greenery and the fact that students there were generally receptive. I made a couple of remarks about Lord of The Rings and sheep but JD sir ignored them.

Ranjana ma'am asked me if I would like another cup of tea, I looked at my wristwatch and realized that I had been sitting with them for more than an hour now. I declined the offer for tea in the best way I could and asked for their leave.

Both JD sir and Ranjana ma'am came to see me off till the end of the lane, JD sir smiled and became ten years younger, I was almost back in school, standing next to him and talking after a class, he said, 'I could see from your face that you are concerned about me. I know, and sometimes I am worried too. But things aren't so bad, besides I have Ranjana with me. It's all going to be alright.' I touched their feet and was about to leave when his son Anmol came, wheeling his cycle next to him. The parents started fussing over him and I slowly exited, moved by JD sir's optimism and at the sight of a family which for one moment did not feel like they had been away from each other for half a decade. Like him, I too had left Baroda, and yet as I stood in the narrow road between my school and the lane from which I had just came out it felt as if I had never really left this city. And this city hadn't left me either.

I had promised Sonam that I would call her up and tell her how my meeting with JD sir had gone. I had earlier told her that since we might not have much to talk about I might be in and out of his house in ten minutes, she was pleased that I had actually stayed for more than an hour.

I told her about JD sir going to New Zealand because of the Internet. She said, 'I knew that, he had told me that he had seen a chance of going to New Zealand to work, and then he had asked me my opinion on whether he should actually go. Vaibhav, for a long time I felt guilty because I told him that he should. And he isn't exactly in a good condition there.'

I mentioned that JD sir would have taken other opinions into account as well, she said, 'Yes, exactly. I later realized that he would have thought of all the pros and cons of what going there would be like. And I was a kid then, I didn't really know any better.'

I told her about the rest of the things, of JD sir being thinner and looking older, about how Sonam was a very hardworking girl, and I could almost see her smile on the other end of the phone, 'Vaibhav, I worry about him at times. He isn't really earning much, do you think he will be okay?'

I had a smile on my face when I realized that I had subconsciously started humming 'New York, New York' once more. When Sonam asked why I had started singing, I said it was nothing (except force of habit) and I repeated what JD sir had told me, if he can make it in Bombay then he sure can make it in New Zealand. And the sparkle in his eyes told me that he would.

THE DIVINE FUNNEL

"**W**hat I am offering you is some sort of a funnel." Narad Muni said as he sat cross-legged on the single bed in Manik's room. "It will help you channelize a million prayers and turn it into one powerful blessing."

Manik did not understand what Narad Muni was giving him. At least it wasn't something that he could see, or touch. "How will that help my brother...how will it cure him?"

"You need the prayers of a thousand people, and all of them should be praying for your brother's health. And this funnel will combine the effects of all their prayers, and will help in healing your brother."

"You mean...like completely? In a flash? Magically?"

Narad Muni smiled, "It's a lot more complex than you think it is. But let me assure you, it will happen sooner than you think."

"So...how do I use this funnel? How does it work? And when do I get it!"

"You already have it, consider it given."

"So what's the procedure for using it? Do I have to say some special mantra? Tell me, I will write it down." Manik quickly tore a fresh page off a notebook.

"No, just meditate and call me, I shall do the needful. But you must be careful in selecting the area where you want to use it."

"That's easy," Manik said, "I will use it over some religious place, like the Golden Temple, or Kashi Vishwanath, or Mecca! Tens of thousands people congregate there and pray. The cumulative effect of their prayers must be huge!"

Narad Muni started playing a tune, this annoyed Manik to such an extent that he wished to take the Muni's instrument and bang him over the head with it. "Narad ji you are not helping!"

"The places you just mentioned are all good, but consider this, do the people that pray there all pray for the same thing?"

Manik thought about it, it was true that even though thousands of people thronged the holy cities together, but they didn't pray for the same thing. Each wanted God to listen to their woes and better their own fortunes. It seemed impossible to find a huge crowd of people who would wish for the same thing.

"Where is such a place where all the people pray for the same thing!?

"Easy, easy my boy." The Muni laughed. "There are a few things you have to remember, first, all the people whose prayers are captured in the funnel should be praying for the same thing, secondly, all the people should be praying around the same time, thirdly, you would get to use it only once, so use it wisely."

"But...how will I find this place? And how do I ensure that all of them are praying for my brother's health? I am not rich enough to host a hawan for this purpose."

"You don't have to, it doesn't matter what the people are praying for if they pray for it with fervour the funnel will change the blessings for their prayers to whatever you want it to be. Of course, their prayers won't be fulfilled, but yours will be. God is generous."

Manik got angry, "If God is so generous then why doesn't He directly heal my brother? I pray to him every day. Why does He want me to use this...this divine funnel?"

Narad Muni got up to leave, "Perhaps She wants to take a test of her disciple."

"She?"

Narad Muni winked and said, "She moves in mysterious ways child." Then without a flash or any sound, he disappeared.

Manik was in a fix, where would he find a place that suited Narad Muni's specifications? There are a million places of worship in the country, but for none could it be said for sure that all the people would pray for the same thing. To de-stress himself he turned on the TV, thinking maybe that will give him some idea.

He stopped at the sports channel, looking at the score of the cricket match between India and Australia.

Australia had scored a massive total of 350, and India had given a good chase, with Sachin leading on at a score of 175 not out. However, they had lost a lot of wickets and were certainly not in a very secure position.

And at precisely that moment Sachin got out, as he did his long walk to the pavilion the camera panned the crowd to capture the anxious and sad faces. They all wished for the same thing, for India to win somehow even though the Master Blaster was gone.

They all prayed for India's victory.

The remote dropped from his hand, he quickly closed his eyes and started meditating to call Narad Muni.

India lost the match by three runs.

27 CAROL

It was a dark and stormy night. Jonathan 'Johnny' Donavan was sleeping fitfully in his bed in an obscure motel room where he had registered under a fake name. He had a big tour coming up starting New Year's Eve and he had had taken leave from the record company to 'recharge his batteries'. Johnny was the flavour of the season, his song *'Better Gear'* was a rage and had reached either the second or third position in charts across all of America, and he had made it to many 'Top Ten Songs of the Year' lists of 1971. He was on the verge of making it big or falling back to obscurity.

Throughout the sixties he had seen many singers and bands becoming One Hit Wonders. He did not want to be labelled one himself and thus wanted to get the most out of his concert tour. On Christmas Eve he had checked into 'Motel Nostalgia', his record company wanted him to be in New York for some PR events, but he wanted to be away from the noise for at least one week before he would be forced to dive head first into it. 'Jus' don't come back dead, man.' His manager Doug had said to him, he was known for his characteristic dry wit and dark humour. These words returned to Johnny in his dreams as he woke up with a start, sweating profusely in the chilly winter night. He wiped the sweat with his right sleeve and noticed that he was shivering. He fumbled around the bed side table for a cigarette to calm his nerves down. He was certain that he was having a nightmare but couldn't quite remember what he had seen.

Black and white images flickered on the TV screen. Johnny noticed that some old western opera was on. He liked to sleep with the TV on and the volume turned down. It made him feel comfortable. He was no longer sweating, yet he felt the need of fresh air. He lifted the only window of his first floor room and inhaled the cool breeze. He instantaneously felt better, as he stood facing outside he forgot about his nightmare. The cool breeze made him want for some bourbon. He had half a bottle on his night stand. He made a small peg and drank it down straight, and made another which he intended to sip slowly. He sat down on the side of his bed and thought of Christmas, of what he wanted to do the next day when he suddenly heard a familiar tune being played on the bass. It was a simple bass line, but the staccato tapping reminded him of someone who he had been close to a long time ago. He turned to see the TV which was definitely on mute. For an irrational reason he was afraid to turn around and see what the source of the music was. His fears were confirmed when he heard a familiar nasal voice singing along with the bass line. 'Merry Christmas everybody, la la la la la la la la la.' The glass in his hand fell down on the floor, and he turned around in disbelief.

'Sarah.' He whispered.

Standing a few feet away from him, leaning against the wall was a young girl with tousled hair. She was wearing a tank top and torn jeans and seemed to be oblivious to the December cold. She was playing a black coloured bass, looking at the notes while she played. She looked up to him and smiled, 'Merry Christmas Johnny Donny, what's the famous singer doing alone on Christmas eve? Couldn't get a girl to fuck?'

Johnny stared at her wide eyed, stammering out words which made no sense. 'Oh spit it out, spit it out, I know the question that you want to ask me.' 'How...how did you come in?' The girl stopped playing the bass and started laughing, she took a step forward and her features started changing. Her face became paler and small streaks of green started appearing across it. 'Johnny Donny, stupid sonny, I think the more important question is whether I'm still alive or not.'

Johnny replied quickly, 'I know that you are dead. Finger called me up and told me. I ...'

'You didn't give a damn about coming to my FUCKING FUNERAL!' Her features had become hideous, the radiance that she had on her face had disappeared and had been replaced by something dangerous and foreboding. She wailed like a banshee for some time making him cover his ears to shield them from the pain, and then she suddenly took a step back, leaned against the wall, resting her left foot against it. Her features relaxed and she became a young beautiful girl again. She picked up her bass guitar and started playing the tune of 'Jingle bells.' 'Pour yourself a drink,' she said, 'It'll help you. And sit down, we need to talk.'

Johnny did as he was told, he was on the verge of complete suspension of disbelief. He sat on the edge of the bed closer to Sarah. He finished his drink in two huge gulps, trying to rationalize what was happening as his awakening from one nightmare to another. 'I know you are not man enough to apologize,' she said, 'so I'm not going to bother with that bullshit. I will just do the task I have been given and be gone.'

'Sarah...why the hostility? I never wanted to hurt you...'

'BE QUIET! Sarah stopped playing the bass, her face showed that she was here against her wishes. 'Now look, I was sent here because I was the closest thing to what you could call a friend. And it is my duty to tell you...'

'You were sent here? Who sent you here? And why?'

Sarah ignored him and continued, 'and it is my duty to tell you that tonight you shall be visited by three gentlemen. Listen to them and perhaps it will help you. I hope it changes you. Actually I don't give a damn if you change or not. To me you will always be a rat.' Before Johnny could even comprehend what was happening, Sarah started dissolving in thin air. Out of instinct he jumped towards her, to touch and check if she was real. By that time only her disembodied face remained. She whispered in a shrill voice, 'And *Better Gear* was MY song!'

Johnny woke up with a headache. He remembered having the most life-like dream of his life. As he rubbed his forehead to relieve himself from the pain, he saw the almost empty bottle of bourbon on the bed side table. He smiled and made a mental note to never buy cheap liquor again. He searched for and replaced the cap of the bottle and decided not to drink again in the night. He lit up a cigarette and walked towards the cabinet on which a jug of water was kept. He drank deeply, trying to wash away the effects of the whiskey.

He thought of Sarah, his childhood friend. She was the first person to have suggested forming a band. Both of them had been self-taught guitarists, starting out by trying to imitate the sounds of Chuck Berry, Elvis and the other greats. Almost ten years ago to the date they had saved some money and bought an electric guitar and a bass. They had flipped a coin to decide who would play which instrument. Sarah was a natural leader, she had quickly recruited three other kids, Thomas Manfried, Gary 'Greedy' Smith and Bill 'Finger' Jones. Thomas was a trained guitarist and he did a lot in improving the skills of the band, and did not mind playing with kids who were really amateur because he personally lacked any sort of creative talent. Greedy, the youngest child of the band had an amazing voice. He had earned his name because he was extremely fat and was literally addicted to food. He sang in a deep voice, but was able to hit the high notes with ease. He was the only one in the band who didn't smoke because he knew what he had was precious. Finger played the drums, and he was brought in by Sarah only because she was blindly in love with him, and because he owned a drum kit. He was a cocky teenager who had given himself this name because he believed that his drumsticks were an extension of his fingers. He wasn't bad, but he was mediocre. And he was very, very simple. His dumbness was just another thing that endeared him to Sarah. Greedy and Thomas more or less hated Finger but Sarah couldn't do without him. And such was her control over the band that they didn't dare question her judgement. Johnny didn't care. All he wanted was for the band to function. Even then he knew that one day he would have to leave this band, and Sarah, behind.

For four years the band played at non-descript venues, often for free. Sarah was against playing at 'social events' like marriages and parties. Instead they played at run down pubs, where all the clientele cared for was that there should be some noise in the background. It wasn't until they broke Sarah's rule and performed at the annual alumni reunion of the local school for a payment that was more than what they had received till now in total, that they started playing for money and they played at whatever occasion paid them.

Johnny was now totally relaxed, he pulled the quilt over him and rested smugly in the bed, mildly happy for the nightmare because although it had wrecked his nerves, it had brought forth a wave of nostalgia. He was almost asleep as his thoughts about his past brought a smile to his face. His mind was at peace. At that exact moment a loud clap of thunder broke his sleep. He heard the sound of an acoustic guitar playing a blues tune. He put it to some guitarist playing in the next room, but at the next crack of lightening, he saw a black man sitting on top of the cupboard, picking at the strings of the guitar expertly. Overwhelmed by this second visitation of the night, he instinctively flicked on the light switch. "Merry Christmas Sonny, A've gotcha present.'

Before Johnny could speak anything, the man threw a small gift box at him.

'Op'n it Sonny, Ah reckin this oughta use of you'

Johnny apprehensively tore apart the gift wrapping of the box, inside it was a well worn wooden guitar pick with the initials 'RJ' on it. 'Who…who are you?'

The man laughed heartily, 'Ah knew you be askin' me this. Ah can't answer this, they tol' me not ta. Ya kin call me Mr Past, if you hafta call me summin', that is.'

Johnny looked at the bottle of liquor, and looked back at the apparition. He was not sure whether he was in another dream or whether the man standing in front of him was real. He couldn't believe that this particular bottle of bourbon could have done so much damage to his brain. 'Y'must be thinkin' that A'm not real, innit? Sonny that pick in yer hand oughta be proof enough.' Mr Past walked closer to him and Johnny saw that there was something very weird about him. The man standing in front of him looked as if he had been photographed in Sepia tone. He heard the man laugh gently, 'Don' be wonderin' why a've been lookin' like this ta you. Tha's jus' how folks remember me, is all.'

'I…I don't remember you. I don't even know who you are!'

'A'h can't blame ya sonny, I's way before your tahme. They don't be singin' my songs much but I been hearin' that lad Clapton, he been playin' my song these days. Playin' it for three years now, you know…' Mr Past played a very familiar blues tune on his guitar, Johnny racked through his brain to search for the song. He had heard this tune a lot, had even tried to play it himself now that he remembered it, but for the life of him he could not figure out which song it was. And when the name of the song came to him, he was awestruck.

'Are you saying…you are the original writer of…'

'A'hm saying we ain't got much tahme with me, a've gotta task at hand and a'h will have ta show you summin'. Come Sonny boy, we gotta hustle.' Mr Past opened the door of the room and exited, not knowing what to do Johnny did the same. 'Now Johnny, be good lad. You'd wanna be payin' tention, don't be wanting to come back 'gain ta this place is what they tol' me. So, fer one final tahme, ye gotta see.'

Outside the door was the garage where Johnny's band practiced. It looked a bit hazy as if covered with thick smog, but it was the same place, Finger was sitting behind the drum kit, Sarah was standing over the remains of a broken bass guitar and the rest of the band stood in a sort of semi-circle around her. 'YOU SON OF A BITCH!' She shouted, and she flung the neck of her bass towards Johnny who ducked just in time.

Greedy came and stood in front of him, shielding him from her, he said in a calm voice, 'We are all pissed off with this asshole Sarah, but it's not worth breaking expensive instruments, you do realize that the only other bass that we have is a…'

'I DON'T GIVE A FUCK! WHO DOES HE THINK HE IS? FUCKING JEFF BECK OR SOMEONE? TWO BIT GUITAR PLAYER!'

Greedy continued, 'In his defence, he hasn't really…' '

IN HIS DEFENCE? YOU WANT TO DEFEND THIS MOTHERFUCKER? YOU WANT TO BE THE NEXT IN LINE AFTER I KILL HIM?' Greedy shrugged and motioned to Finger, as if saying, 'Take care of your girl man!' He reluctantly got up from behind the drums, as if he was leaving his place of safety. He tried to fold her in a comforting hug, and this was when she started crying, sobbing softly into the shoulders of her boyfriend. Johnny remained impassive; the other two band members turned to him and told him that this was the point where he should quietly exit. 'But don't take the 1955 Gibson,' Manfried said, 'It was bought with the band's money and not yours. Take away your other gear though. But you have no right to take the better gear.'

Johnny took his time packing his stuff, showing no emotion. Greedy took out a bag of candy from his pocket and munched on them noisily. Manfried picked up the pieces of the broken bass and put them away while Sarah cried in sporadic jerks. As Johnny was about to leave she called out to him, 'John wait…' She went up to him and spoke softly, almost in a whisper, 'I know why you are leaving…' She waited for him to answer, and when he didn't she continued, 'it's because of that dumb fuck Finger isn't it.' She turned and stared at the drummer who at that moment was playing the part of Dumb-Fuck quite convincingly.

'Not so loud…' Johnny spoke for the first time, 'He is right here.'

'So what! So fucking what! I don't care about him John, I care about you.' She kept her hand on his chest, grasping his shirt lightly.

'Then why was he in the band in the first place? And don't worry, I am not leaving because of your sex toy, I think I have reached a point in life where I really have to go forward.'

'I have heard your crappy speech before,' Sarah stopped him, 'only…I thought you were joking.' 'Well in any case, let's keep Finger out of it, and let's just say that I am quitting because I feel like it.'

Sarah fixed him with a stare and spoke in a slow voice, 'Don't give me this vague bullshit John, I think there is an exact reason for you leaving…you are not leaving, this is blackmail. You want something else don't you?' Johnny was silent, suddenly, Sarah became wide eyed. 'Oh my God!' She said, 'You bastard! You fucking bastard! You ARE leaving because of Finger.'

'I don't know what you are talking about.'

'Yes! You are jealous.'

'Of that incompetent tone deaf fool?'

'Jealous…because he gets to fuck me!'

'You are crazy!' Johnny shot back violently.

'So this is what will keep you in the band, isn't it? Well come on then sugar, fuck me! I'm gonna let you have sex with me, you no good guitarist..'

'Leave me!' Johnny jerked her hand away, she gripped the cloth of his shirt tight, making it get torn across his chest.

'FUCK ME!' She shouted after him as he hurriedly left the room, 'FUCK ME YOU GODDAMNED BASTARD! IT'S WHAT YOU HAVE ALWAYS WANTED!' Johnny closed the door behind him, drowning out the banshee screams of his erstwhile band mate.

'That there was some touchy scene innit boy,' Mr Past stroked his chin thoughtfully. Johnny had not liked revisiting this memory,

'Why did you bring me here Mr Past?'

'Weeel, ah'd ta aks ye a veery portant question.'

'Look Mr Past, if you want to know, I left the band because they were dragging me down. And I told them so, although not in such direct words.'

'He he he, A've gotta tell ye da truth. Ah feilt the same way about my band, but in yer case lad, a've gotta feeling, you aint tellin the truth te nobody, not me not that fine lass there. And ah tell ya, that's one fine lass. You do her, ever?' He finished with a low wolf whistle.

'What! No! Never, we were such good friends, I never...
never even thought...'

'Ye can't fool no-one, know. Got a veiry transparent face
there, you lie, you did want to do her. And this other kid, plays
drum like some drunk white boy, he getting to do her when
he wants. Didn't like that?' Johnny chose to not reply. Instead
he asked, 'When will you take me back home?' Mr Past gave
him a very toothy smile, and slowly started dissolving in the air
around him, 'A'hd come to take ye back home boyo, tis upto ye
if ye wanna go back.'

When Donavan awoke again, he had the wooden guitar
pick in his hand, telling him that the visitation of the guitarist
was no dream. He rationalized to himself that perhaps he had
been drugged, as part of some conspiracy and that the bottle of
bourbon was what was used. He quickly got up from the bed
and picked the bottle from the bed side table, determined to
empty its contents. He knew that the whole thing was some trick
of light or some medicines; although that black man really might
have been present there, but what he showed him, would have
had to be a hallucination which was guided by some drug. He
went to the open window and threw the bottle towards a vacant
lot, not giving a damn who heard the noise. The bottle careened
and disappeared into the darkness, ending its trajectory with a
loud shattering noise. Donavan next took the pick in his hand
and was about to throw it, but then decided against it, he put it
inside his jeans pocket. He nervously searched the small room,
armed with an electric guitar, he peered inside the bathroom,
looked behind the shower curtain and went to the extent of
checking the cupboard to see if anyone hid inside. He cautiously
tip-toed to the hotel corridor outside and checked if all the doors
were closed. He thought of going down to the reception and
complaining, but then decided against it. It would be hard to
prove to a half-asleep hotel clerk that he had a visitation from a
ghost, or a thief, especially when nothing was stolen. He came

back to his room, secured the main door and the bathroom door, shut the window tightly and decided to give sleep another shot. As soon as he had almost drifted off, he heard a low whizzing noise next to his ear as something flew above him and crashed into the wall in front.

He got up, more alert but all the more scared this time and shouted 'Dammit! Where are you! Show yourself! Mr Past?'

Standing a few feet away with his face towards the wall was a thin, lanky young man wearing a leather jacket, he had a bottle of Jack Daniels in one hand, and was waving the other one around drunkenly, he said, 'Settle down ladies and gentlemen… the show as you call it is about to begin…the stunned demons are at their lives end…and if you want to know what to call me, I am Mr Present.'

Donavan rubbed his face with his palms; he closed his eyes tightly, trying to shut out this nightmare that he now knew he was going through. He muttered 'Oh God…Oh God…Oh God' under his breath when suddenly he heard the sound of an electric guitar, coming through a very dirty distortion. It was a strange and beautiful sound and he recognized its pattern immediately. His eyes shot up to see that the thin man with the bottle of JD had been replaced by another thin man with an impressive afro and a guitar being played the other way round. He took a few small steps to where the man was standing, and wondered whether he should bother asking if this was a dream or should he fetch his autograph book. For all he knew, the man standing in front of him was a dead man, a ghost, and here he was, in his hotel room playing. 'Are…are…are…you real?' The visitation did not reply, instead he started playing a slow and heavy rhythm on his guitar, preferring not to speak. Donavan took a few steps more, gingerly reaching out a hand towards the spirit when suddenly, there was white noise, the image flickered and the man with the Jack Daniels was back. He quickly climbed the cupboard in front, still facing away from Donavan and said 'What is real, my friend….come, I will take you to see your intended end…or at least the presumed end for me…come and tell me, do you see what I see.' Donavan almost fell back when he saw this sudden change, and when the man in front of him turned around and jumped back down, he too was easily recognizable. Two dead icons, a single manifestation of both of them, and it was John Donavan's luck that they had decided to descend upon him. 'Do you…do you too have something to show me?' Even before he could finish speaking, the guitarist was back. And this time it seemed that he played with immense concentration, so that the sound coming from some unseen source almost seemed solid. The sound enveloped Donavan, it caught him tightly as if a thick mattress had been rolled across his body. Donavan half fought it as he was carried away.

When Donavan regained his senses he found out that he was back in his old town, he seemed to be floating in mid-air above a crowd. He recognized the place as an all-night pub, one of the first places that allowed their band to play and even paid them a frugal fees. He scanned the place for signs to tell him what day it was, when he heard the voice of the singer of the band playing there presently. It was Greedy. He turned to look at the stage and saw a band desperately trying to keep it together for a half-drunk half-asleep audience. Thomas too was there, although the drummer and bass guitarist were people Donavan had never seen. The drummer looked like a 15-year-old kid. Greedy and Thomas had started the song well until the drums kicked in, when all things went haywire. The drummer was soaked, and he had a hard time keeping even a flat monotonous rhythm going. The bass guitarist pretended to play for a while and then decided that there was no use making an effort, so he started playing random disjointed notes.

When Donavan could not bear watching he turned to the guitarist and asked, 'Look, look at them, can't you do something? Maybe some magic to help them! You are the best guitarist the world ever had, and even in your death you still...' The guitarist looked at him with sad eyes and shrugged, as if to say that this was beyond him. Donavan turned to the stage again to see Greedy ducking to save himself from projectiles being thrown by the audience. Thomas had already disappeared, Greedy too jumped awkwardly off stage and went and hid into the kitchen of the place. 'Why have I been brought here?' Donavan thought aloud.

'You need to see...' The thin man had returned, 'That as big as you can be...you are never bigger than your band...do you realize!' The man suddenly caught hold of Donavan's collar in a strong grip and shook him violently. 'I...I was hungry too, perhaps more than you...but I was never, and I mean never bigger than them!' He waved his hand towards the now empty stage. Before Donavan could say anything, the thin man shouted 'You disgust me! Get away from me!' And he threw him towards the stage.

Donavan landed with a thud on his bed. His head hurt, and his body ached from the impact. He got up again and looked around for further ectoplasmic presence in his room. When he was sure that there was no one there, he got up and lit a cigarette, pacing around the room as he smoked.

After almost an hour had passed he concluded that a new ghost will appear only when he has his eyes closed or if he is partially asleep. With this logic he lay down on his bed again, waiting for sleep to come. It felt like he had been asleep for a long time when he was woken not by a guitar sound but by a hand roughly shaking his shoulder. Standing in front of him was a man he had never seen before. He seemed to be roughly his own age, but was wearing clothes that seemed weird. His shirt was many sizes too big for him and his jeans were torn at several places. He too had a guitar case slung over his shoulder. 'Wake up man, wake up!' He said while he continued to shake him. Donavan sat up and rubbed the sleep off his eyes, he asked him, although he knew this question was useless, 'Who are you?' He knew who the two (one?) men who had visited him just before and Mr Past too seemed to have been someone famous at a point in time. This young man with long blond hair and ill-fitting clothes he could not seem to place. 'You…you do not seem to be familiar.'

'I am already here, but I in myself am not here anymore. You do not know me yet, and if things do not plan out well, you will join our club and yet never know who I am. I have come from the future, and if you want to see it, you need to come with me.'

This time Donavan was genuinely scared, 'What! What do you mean? Am I to die soon? Why won't I see the future…'

'Never mind. Just come with me, come as you are.'

For the third time in the same night Donavan was teleported, and this time he was standing in a cemetery. He spoke in a scared, stammering voice, 'Why have you brought me here?'

'Do you want me to be curt and tell you the truth?'

'Yes…yes please.'

The man from the future started walking slowly in front of him, he spoke in a measured voice, 'A few days from now you shall have a series of concerts. These concerts will establish you as a big music star throughout the country. You will not notice it because you would not care, that your fan base has shifted. What people will start expecting from you are electronic sounds and candy coated lyrics. You will happily oblige them, raking in more and more money. Within a few months you will stop even touching your guitar, relying on a new wave of 'producers', who will synthesize your music for you. Soon you shall be responsible for the beginning of the decline of the music that you love. One fine day, in fact just before your birthday, in a drunken haze you will have a…what you call it…an epiphany making you realize what you have done. It will never be clear if your drug and alcohol overdose is intentional or not.' The man had walked up to a grave and stopped, it was too dark for them to see whose grave it was.

'It's too…too dark…' Donavan said as he went close to the headstone.

'It's less dangerous with the lights out.' The man offered, 'I don't have a torch, and even though I have been given this task, I really don't want you to see this…' Dramatically a car went by the cemetery, and its headlight flashed on the headstone. Johnny Donavan's worst fears were confirmed. He fell on his knees, aware of the tears rolling down his face. 'Please…please tell me…'

The man sighed and sat down next to him, 'There is no tenderness associated with this death John. After your death you will be eaten up by obscurity. Others, far too greater died around the same time, and in front of them, despite the monstrosities that you will record, you shall not have the fame' he almost spat out the word, 'Johnny Donavan, you shall not be remembered.'

Donavan cried silently, against all hope he wished that this was some nightmare which would end with the night. The man got up and gave him his guitar case, he started walking away, 'There are three things you can do. You can use what's in the guitar case, you can go down to where you came from, or you can ignore this night. And do what you will do in any case.' He turned back once and said, 'Just promise me one thing, if you come for me when it's my time, you will bring that guitar case. Merry Christmas John.' He disappeared, and the place around him started to go hazy. Johnny clutched the guitar case as he waited to be teleported back to his hotel room.

John Donavan woke up on the morning of Christmas, he felt weirdly fresh even though it had seemed to him that he had hardly slept through the night. He looked around and saw that the bottle of bourbon was gone, and that there was lesser number of cigarettes in the pack that he had. The final confirmation of the night's events being true came when he saw a wooden pick lying next to his pillow, and a guitar case on the ground. He slowly opened the guitar case, it had a sawed off shotgun inside it. He immediately closed the case as he realized the true import of what the man from the future had said. He kicked the guitar case away in horror. 'No…' he said to himself, 'I won't…' He moved on his own, without meaning to. He could see his hands opening the case and taking the shot gun out of it. He could now see himself staring down the barrel of the gun, he saw flashes of the images he had seen last night. He saw Sarah shouting at him for leaving the band, he saw Greedy breaking down on stage, he saw his own headstone and presently he felt the cold metal of the trigger, he closed his eyes, trying to think of a happy thought, the last thing he would think of before blowing his brains off. He thought of Sarah. And suddenly, the rest was easy.

John Donavan checked out of the hotel room after a few hours, he stopped at a pay phone near a bus station. 'This is Johnny here, I wanna speak to Doug, Doug Adams.' After a while his manager came on the phone, 'Johnny my boy. Your R&R over? Coming home tonight?' Donavan laughed and said, 'No Doug, I am GOING home tonight. I am sorry I broke your promise, but I am a dead man. And I can't come back.' 'You high motherfucker?' 'You bet I am.' 'Look…I don't have time for jokes, John…Johnny?' Donavan had hung up the phone, he smiled as he thought of his destination. After a while he found out that he was humming, and he was pleasantly surprised to realize that he was singing *Better Gear*.

THE BOOK KEEPER

I met Suniel when I joined a new sales job in one of India's indigenous cell phone manufacturing companies. It was a job which involved a lot of travelling between three of India's major cities---Mumbai, Delhi and Kolkata. And on each of these visits if I was accompanied by Suniel, he would make it a point to visit second hand bookshops, near Flora Fountain in Mumbai, in Daryaganj in Delhi and at College Street in Kolkata.

It did not seem to me to be a particularly weird obsession since I too liked buying good old books if I could get them at discounted price, but Suniel was different, in fact it would be an understatement to call him weird. He generally bought almost three to four books on each of his visits, and with the job requiring him to visit every city once a month he bought more than ten books a month. I never saw him reading any of those books, even during the long and arduous train journeys we had to undertake at times, all I saw was him was typing away on his weather beaten Dell laptop. Once I asked him to pique my curiosity, 'Suniel bhai, do you get to read all these books that you buy?'

He laughed and said, 'It doesn't take a lot of time for me to read the books. It takes around fifteen twenty minutes for me to go through them.'

'But even the best of speed-reading can't make you read around 200 pages in twenty minutes, what are you, Clark Kent?'

'No…never mind, forget what I said.' And he went back to typing in his laptop.

I still accompanied him to his book buying outings to see if there was some special pattern of books which he bought, because I had seen many such 'book collectors' who buy a particular type of book, and do not necessarily read it, be it the second world war, or autobiographies of world leaders or even obscure pulp fiction. But Suniel's book buying had no such pattern either. The only peculiar thing was that he would read the first page of the book, weigh it in his hand for a couple of seconds and then make his decision.

I became obsessed with his own obsession. I made it a personal quest to know why he bought books in such a quantity if he never appeared to read them. 'Do you sell them further?' I asked him, 'Do you have some sort of a lending library? Why do you buy them if you don't read them?'

'I buy them for the stories they give me…' And he would repeat his claim about being able to read a book in record time.

'Shouldn't you go on one of those Guinness Record shows if you can do what you claim?'

He got slightly angry, 'Why is this so important to you? Let me be, and let my books be. Besides, public attention is the least of what I crave, at least right now.'

I invited myself to a weekend Bring Your Own Beer party at his apartment, just to see what he does with his books and to catch him in an inebriated state and get the truth out of him. Unfortunately for me he turned out to be a very light drinker, and with the doses of Kingfisher Strong that I plied upon him, he went out too quickly.

I searched around his house and saw regular books, not his 'second-hand' collection, but mostly new books. It took me some time to find a hidden rack in one of the two inner rooms, it looked like a normal cupboard but was in fact a book shelf, and it had over two hundred books, more than half of them properly covered with plastic and all of them labelled with a strange marking system, like some librarians code. The books were not kept alphabetically, but the tags on them were alphabetical, all books tagged 'A-Ab-An-As-...' etc. were kept together in a series, but their names had no relation that seemed apparent to me at that time. I realized I too was a bit drunk and decided that I would ask him again in the morning.

He was rather cross when I told him I had discovered his book set, 'Well now you must be satisfied that I am not selling these books as a side-business.' 'But you do seem to keep a library of sorts, and why the strange labelling? And what about all those that are covered in plastic?' He sighed and said, 'If I tell you, you would think that I am some sort of a freak.' 'But I already think of you as some sort of freak!' 'Then I guess there is no use telling you, is there?'

I later realized that it was not right on my part to barge in on his privacy like that and apologized. I stopped asking him about his book collection and book buying too, although the thought remained in my mind, nagging me continuously. I avoided going with him when he went to buy the books and stopped any mention of his habit.

But one day I relented and went with him again to a bookshop, he asked me categorically if I was going to pester him with questions again, and I refused, promising him I would not be bothering him. I had every intention of keeping my promise.

There was a time when the book shops near Flora fountain were quite extensive and were spread to a distance of about one kilometre, almost up to the Churchgate station. Now the shops are scattered in pockets of the Fort area, except for one corner near Hutatma Chowk that has around six or seven such independent establishments that remind you of the glory of these second hand book sellers. The prices too are not what they used to be, around ten years ago you could get a decent book for under fifty rupees if you drove a hard bargain but the knowledge of these 'independent' book sellers has increased with time, and they know which books are available at a steep price in the market which a customer would be willing to pay for, and they make it a point to tell you that they are charging you less than half of what you would have to shell out in a shop. Suniel went to the particular shop which he frequented, and as a result would get an additional Rs. 10 discount per book on sheer goodwill, he had never had to ask for it. The shopkeeper acknowledged him with a small nod and asked one of his workers to bring forth a huge stack of books, as was his practice when Suniel came to the shop, these books were not filtered by author or genre or anything. Suniel would thumb them, pick out a few, read the first page at times, hold them in his hands and then make his decision, at times buying three and at times buying four. I made it a point to mentally block what he was doing and busied myself in selecting a book; in fact I too bought one, an old spy thriller by an American author for reading in the train.

However, once inside our AC 2 coupe, I could not resist myself and asked him, 'Suniel bhai, once you said that you can read a book in twenty minutes.'

He kept aside his laptop and said, 'Look, it's not what it sounds like, and if I tell you how...anyway you promised me that you would let this topic be, why suddenly this...'

'Actually I too bought a book today, and I thought maybe if you could show me how you do your speed reading etc...'

'It's not some kind of magic show, well I mean, actually it is...but...look I am only telling you this because you pester me so much and…besides it depends on the book' By then I had already taken out the book from my briefcase and handed it over to him, he took it reluctantly and kept it on the small table in front of him. I said, 'Come on, please, you know if you tell me what you really do with these books I will stop asking you these questions in the first place.'

He said, 'Ok…Ok…I have actually told this to a few friends of mine, and apart from that no one has really been that nosey in my life, but promise me that you won't tell anyone what I show you today. At least not till I am ready.'

I had no idea about what was going to happen next, literally none. He took the book in his hand, I heard him whispering 'How did I miss this one?' as he opened and read the first page. Then he began 'This book that you gave me today has actually crossed more than four pair of hands, how much did you pay for it, Rs 50? Ah ! yes I can see that small pencil mark on the last page, it signifies that the shopkeeper had decided to sell it for a minimum of that much, when you have studied such books as I have you tend to notice such things. The first page has a note inscribed *Major Pradeep Mum/1984*, this is not a gift from someone, Major sa'ab bought it for himself. In fact he bought it at Strand, for twenty, not far from where you re-bought it today. The Major was a fan of spy thrillers and he fancied himself to be part of one, although he only got to see 'action' when he had to against his wishes be part of the attack on Golden Temple. All the while this book was with him in his satchel, as he sat in Military trucks or when he took a train to comeback to Delhi for debriefing, and it was on a train similar to this that he misplaced his satchel and this book and some other contents of that bag were lost forever to him. He spent some time searching for it, not because the book was dear to him, but perhaps there was something else in that bag, what was it? A gift from a loved one or something else? In any case the bag was found by another young man on the train who promptly interred it into the 'Lost and Found' segment at the station masters office but kept the book for himself, since he had a long journey to make still, a bus ride and then a tractor ride along with his father who did not look too kindly towards his habit of reading fiction. The book stayed with the young man for some years, although he did not keep it entirely with affection, in fact during the last year of his Engineering college he gave the book to a friend whom he had borrowed money from, and was not entirely in a position of returning. That friend of his shifted to Mumbai as his job demanded it, and he too did not have a particular interest for this book. It lay on his shelf for many years when once on a lark, and because he needed a Rs 20/- note to buy four cigarettes, he sold it promptly to the book shop that you have bought it from. And presently, this book is in my hand. This, my friend is the Story of This book. And it took me around ten minutes to read it, because it did not have as many events as I expected it to have in its life till now.'

I was stunned, but then I found voice and laughed lightly, 'Well it's quite apparent that you made that all up, or perhaps you fancy yourself as some new age Sherlock Holmes, who can tell everything about a book just by looking at it.'

He said, 'No, no there is no science of deduction involved, it's much simpler than that. To tell you the truth, which you will scarcely believe, it all comes to me in a vision, and I am not saying that it necessarily happens but...'

'Wait a minute, so you are telling me that once you grab a book in your hand you get visions of what's happened to it in the past?'

'You can say that...although it's not something exact, I get major points, I mean almost from the book's point of view, and then I fill in the blanks with my assumptions.'

'You are some kind of magician, why don't you promote this act of yours on, you know, TV or the Internet or something?'

He sat back and returned the book to me, 'I don't want to be labelled a freak, at least not now, not so soon, you see,' he turned his laptop towards me, 'I have been writing down the stories of all the books that I have come across, most of them are mundane but some are interesting, and I intend to get them published sometime in the future, as a collection of tales, of...'

'But...if what you say is true, how did it start in the first place? And why only books? Why not this laptop or a pen or... anything at all!'

'I guess it's because these books which have changed hands absorb stories as they go along, being for their first purpose papers with stories in them, they act as some kind of sponge, and it all gets released when I hold them.'

Although what he was telling me explained a lot, his collection, his weird obsession and everything, I found it really really hard to believe, I said, 'Look, I know I have pestered you a lot so that you come clean and tell me why you collect these books, but I didn't know you would come up with such an incredulous tale, I mean all I get is that you are a good story teller who...' He sighed, 'I have nothing to gain from lying to you. Honestly, I too thought that what I was getting were images in my overworked mind, even though it happened repeatedly with me. But after the first few instances I decided to investigate, there was this particular cook book that I bought from Darya Ganj once...' 'You mean you like buying cooking books too?'

'That's beside the point, I bought it because I was thumbing through several books and felt something when I touched this one, it had the name Vinita written on the inner cover with a sketch pen, and I had visions of an old woman using the book for its recipes happily and being quite attached to it, and the next scene I saw was of the book being sold by a young man to a *kabaadi*, who was intelligent enough to know that the monetary value it had was of more than its weight, so he promptly resold it to a book shop.'

'I don't get it, how does any of this prove that these visions of yours are real? This Vinita you talk about might easily be a young woman who herself sold the book once she saw that she had no further use of it.'

'I used my visions to track the old lady, she lived in an obscure colony in West Delhi. And I was successful in it. And what she told conformed to what I saw in my mind, her son had sold that book by mistake along with a stack of old newspapers.' I remained silent for a while, contemplating all he had told me, and since I was in a mood for argument I asked him. 'Let us for the time being agree to what you are telling me, but then this...strangeness...doesn't it make you a voyeur? You have free access to multiple lives, to intimate moments, to relationships in fact! And to top it all, you are writing everything you see and you wish to publish it. Don't you think it would be an invasion of privacy?' He countered, 'Isn't every writer a voyeur of some sort? And don't worry, I am not going to use original names, even if people read their own story all they will feel would be a sense of Déjà vu.'

To me the whole thing seemed weird, it was quite possible that everything that Suniel was telling me was a lie, but if it was true it was a fascinating prospect. And I told him clearly that although I had trouble believing in what he said, I did not wish to doubt him so I would take his word for it, besides, he really did not have anything to gain from lying to me.

But then, an incident happened in College Street that made me change my views.

Unlike the quite open corner near Flora Fountain or the shops on the wide road of Darya Ganj, the bookshops of College street sell their collections from tiny shops filled to capacity with books from the sides of a narrow and busy road, it seems almost magical when what looks to be a collection of hundred books or so turns out to be much more than that. I had accompanied Suniel again, and after he had revealed his 'powers' to me, his habit of buying books in a seemingly random pattern came as quite natural. I did not trouble my mind by wondering whether he was telling the truth or not, in fact I actually enjoyed it when he occasionally told some of the stories to me. I did not experiment with him after that day in the train, but then I saw a book, a fairly new old copy of 'Midnight's Children', I had been meaning to buy this title for a long time, so I immediately bought it, I imagined being Suniel and weighed the book in my hand, preparing to spin a story around it, I opened the front cover but was disappointed to see that the inner cover was torn. I showed this to him, because this particular book had no inner cover, it had no handwritten names or dedications, so I thought it would be interesting to see if he had a vision in the absence of a name to guide him.

As I handed the book to him he said, 'Well there's a reason that I normally buy books with something handwritten on the inner cover, I guess the starting point of the story is always the name inscribed in front of the book, I have at times had books without names or with the first pages torn, but then the images in my mind that come are always hazy.' He eyed the book keenly, raising it above his head and then bringing it down, flipping through its pages and playfully sniffing them and then he started speaking, 'This book was given by a guy to a girl who had little interest in them, she tried reading it once but couldn't finish it, I wonder why...this is such a good book...so anyway she offloaded this book to a...to a...wait a minute!' He frantically started turning the pages of the book as if searching for something important, he fingered the edges of the torn remains of a sticker, perhaps looking for a clue to the original book-seller. He continued in a bewildered voice, 'and then she forgot about the book...forgot the fact that it was a gift...while the guy she offloaded it to give it to someone else...and then to someone else...and then it got plain...why did she do this to me!'

Suniel, always weird when telling these tales was acting positively strange this time around, I asked him, 'Are you okay?' Perhaps the strain of these visions had finally started telling on him, and whatever magic was making him have them was beginning to wear off. 'Suniel, do you need something?' In a far-away voice he said, 'This...this is a book I gave to my girlfriend, and I thought she would...but she didn't even read it and it has ended...I mean it's...' As soon as I realized what he was saying I started laughing loudly, I don't know why I did, it was the worst that I could have done at that spot, but in that open street with Suniel dazed and confused on his knees clutching the book in his hand, I stood in front of him and laughed. I laughed at the absurdity of this joke, and also realizing that all this while Suniel had been telling the truth.

For a long time after that Suniel didn't talk to me and I too avoided him when I realized my mistake, although it was too late for me to mend bridges with him, I came to know through common friends that Suniel---The Book Keeper---had stopped collecting books. Nobody knew the reason but me, it was because he had read his own story in a book, and it wasn't one with a happy ending.

ASHOK INTERNATIONAL TEA SHOP

For many years I had been coming to this tea shop regularly on every Friday, and not because of the peculiar name it had (for which Ashok had only one explanation, he had gotten it from a cousin who ran a shop on *Assi Ghat* and used the word International to attract tourists), neither was the tea great. The place stank of urine because of it being adjacent to a toilet, and there were no permanent seating arrangements, just a couple of wooden planks on stone piles that Ashok's mute assistant picked up from the rubble and garbage nearby. Ashok made his tea in the space beneath a stair case that lead to literally nowhere since the building that it was part of had been closed (and open for lease without any takers) for exactly ten years. Apart from tea the only thing that Ashok served were somewhat suspicious quality biscuits which he kept in a filthy glass jar. His main business was cigarettes, where he charged a decent price margin over the market price.

I used to come here because this shop, located in an obscure corner of a shopping complex in *Hathua* Market, was the place where all my friends gathered every evening from seven to eight thirty drinking copious amounts of tea and smoking, hidden from family members and friends of family members (who could be easily met in Benares, whether you liked it or not), but then slowly people either left or got married. I continued coming here, out of a sense of habit, and then later when I made friends with God.

This God fellow has been my friend for almost three to four years now. And I don't know his name, I doubt if he knows mine. The familiarity exists between us because of Ashok's shop. He was the only person whom I had seen drinking only tea and never smoking. This irked Ashok, and felt odd to my group of friends, and that is the first name that we gave him, 'Odd.'

It was after a while when I limited my personal visits to Friday, it pleased me to see the Odd man sitting there comfortably, balancing a cup of tea on his knee and reading a mouldy newspaper. It gave me a sense of familiarity, an old, regular face, who sat there minding his own business. He always folded the paper neatly so that others could read it.

Once, out of sheer boredom, I asked him 'Is there anything worthwhile in the paper that makes you read it? Doesn't news depress you?'

The man smiled and said, 'It's my job to know. And I like the way these papers tell the news.'

I have a brother-in-law who is a police officer, and this man kind of echoed his views. He too loved to read only the Hindi dailies, he had told me 'Most of the news in the paper is bullshit, like that story of a buffalo entering someone else's tabela and there being a huge hue and cry over it, but it takes a keen eye to spot the real news and separate it from the garbage, and that is why I prefer reading the local paper.'

I tried to keep the conversation going, 'Have you shifted to Benares recently? Or have you shifted to Hathua Market?'

He said, 'No I have lived in Banaras for all my life, and yeah I have started frequenting this area off late, I used to hang out around Dashashwmedh, but not anymore. Some friend of mine told me about this little shop, I came here, I liked the general chatter that used to go around here, and I stayed.'

I laughed and told him, 'It's good that you stayed. Hardly anybody that I know comes to this shop these days. All I have for company is the constant bickering of Ashok and his father.' There was a time when there was a strict bifurcation of business, Ashok made and sold tea plus he had control over the biscuits, while his father looked after the selling of cigarettes, paan masala, pass pass, etc. Recently Ashok had wrested total control from his father, citing his old age and inability to keep a proper ledger. His father had relented, although he still insisted on coming to the shop, like me, out of force of habit.

Every Friday the man would be present there, he drank exactly three cups of tea, paid with a note of Rs. 10, was generous enough to let Ashok keep the Re.1 change instead of accepting a pass pass sachet, and he stayed for exactly one hour.

Once I reached before him and picked up the paper, I was reading one of the inner pages with news about fallen trees and light outages, when the man came. I did not realize it then but later I saw that for the duration that I had the paper with me he fidgeted nervously. When I noticed it I offered the paper to him, however, unfortunately at the same time in a rare display of carelessness, Sheetal dropped an entire *purva* of chai on the paper, making it completely drenched and unfit for reading. The paper itself was not of good quality and immediately turned into pulp.

'Well most of it was pulp fiction in any case,' I laughed, but the man did not take to my joke lightly. He stared at me angrily as if saying that I had just now ruined an entire hour of his life. I lit up a Gold Flake and decided it would be best to ignore him,

I picked up my mobile phone and started playing a game on it when he suddenly asked me, 'So what is it that you do?'

'Excuse me?'

'I am sorry, but I need to kill time for an hour, and since I don't have the paper, I guess I will talk to you.'

I wanted to say something sarcastic to thank him for his condescension, but instead I found myself replying, 'I work in the marketing division of a bank' and proceeded to explain to him the nature of my work.

'And what about you?' I asked him.

'I take care of people, at least I try to.'

'You mean you are a Doctor?'

'No...a Doctor is someone who comes in to the picture only when something bad has happened to them, my job is to prevent something bad from happening.'

I was intrigued, 'So do you run a security agency of some sort?'

'You can say that,' he replied with a sly smile, 'only it's a One Man security agency, and I have to take care of the whole world.' He suddenly looked as if he had said something foolish. Perhaps he was exaggerating, as a Banarasi is prone to do, what I guess he meant was that he ran a pan Banaras security agency.

I asked him where his office was and he replied 'Nowhere'. I was now sure that this man is slightly high, and sniffed without letting him know to check for the smell of alcohol and *ganja*. The man then proclaimed simply, 'Actually, I am God.'

I laughed to his face and said, 'Yeah, right, and which God are you? Considering that we have so many.'

He smiled and said, 'I know it's very hard to believe, especially for you, you are an atheist.'

'No, it's hard to believe because it's a joke, right?'

165

'It's not a joke, but it is something that you won't believe because you don't want to.' Saying this he left, he had no newspaper to read and thus nothing to do.

When I was leaving, Ashok asked me why that other man had left quickly, I started saying, 'He is some weird fellow, he claims that he is…' and then checked myself. Perhaps there was something wrong with the guy and that is why he was behaving oddly. There was no reason for me to spread whatever he said about himself.

The next week too I reached before him, this time I was determined to find out who he really was. And that is why I again took possession of the paper and waited for him. When he came I said, 'God *sa'ab*, I was just reading about what is happening in *your* world, but then you must already know about it. Why do you need the paper?'

I thought this might provoke him, but he said nothing and calmly sat down, he ordered tea and a biscuit and waited for Sheetal to serve and leave before he said, 'It is impossible for me to keep a track of everything, unlike popular perception I literally cannot be everywhere and every place at all the time. Those who propagated these beliefs went for over simplification.'

'Still…doesn't mean you need the paper…'

'Let me complete, you see when we have something that does not warrant a plausible explanation, we deal with it by exaggerating it. Where is God? Everywhere! How powerful is God? All Powerful! What does God know? Everything.'

I stopped him and said, 'It sounds like you are the one who is an atheist. And yet you claim to be God, still?'

He smiled and replied, 'Anybody can have moments of self-doubt. Never mind that, I read the paper because I have people working for me in many newspaper companies around the world, and this is how I communicate with them.'

'Go on' I said, 'God or not, you are telling me an interesting tale.'

'Never mind, I tend to get carried away at times. Just give me the paper when you read it before Sheetal drops tea on it again.'

I didn't talk to him on that day after that, but next week when I met him again he continued his claims of being God. 'It's not like you are the first person that I have told this to.' He said, 'I have told this to a few people before, and like you I know that they would not tell anyone. After all, who would believe them?' He laughed like a child. 'Have you told anyone? I guess not.'

I told him, 'It's not that I actually believe that you are God. So why would I tell anyone. You are just someone who is stretching a joke too far.'

'Why would I joke about myself?'

'I don't know, and I frankly do not care.'

The man stared hard at me, and said in a slightly menacing voice, 'Do you want me to show you a magic trick or something?'

I waved my hand and said, 'Don't be angry, I have nothing to gain or lose from believing whether you are, God or not. So be it, let me assume that you are God, and from now on I shall call you so.'

He stayed silent for what seemed like a long time, then exhaled saying 'It's not that it would actually make a difference to me...'

'Cigarette?' I offered, to which he politely declined.

For the next couple of weeks I could not go to Ashok's shop because of some work of my own. It had been almost a month since the man had started his charade, and I thought a couple of weeks would be enough time to forget about it. But still, to break the ice the next time I met him I asked, 'So how are you Mr God?'

167

The man handed me the newspaper and said, 'Look at the tragedy printed on the first page. I feel bad when things like this happen. I try to prevent it, but then…there are too many variables.'

I scanned the news, it was indeed a tragedy, with the death of many people. I responded without really thinking, 'You are the creator. Aren't you responsible for everything that happens around here? So is it not your fault?'

He became angry, 'How is it my fault! All I did was create human beings, I never imagined them to be this way! I didn't know that they would turn into terrorists, murderers! How is it always my fault?' He was almost shaking with anger, and dramatically I saw that dark clouds gathered in the sky above. I smiled when I noticing the coincidence and said, 'Calm down, I am sorry. I did not mean to offend you. Here, sit down and have a cigarette.'

'I don't smoke!' He half-shouted and sat down. I asked Sheetal to bring tea for him, while I lit my cigarette and sat down on the wooden plank opposite to him. I asked him again, 'Tell me, who are you, really?'

The man looked dejected and said, 'I have told you once, and my answer does not change with time. I am not human.'

I wondered who he was for a while and then I asked him, 'Are you a method actor? Is there some movie shooting going on in Banaras? If you are, then hats off man. You are doing a good job.'

The man declined tea and left again.

The next time he met me he looked apologetic, 'I am sorry, I should not have shouted at you the last time. But when I see something I made going wrong, and in case of humans this happens on a very frequent basis, I get emotional.' He showed me the paper and in one of the pages was a small news about a disabled boy who had become a chess champion in his school, 'But when I see things like this it gladdens me. My faith in humanity gets restored a little.'

I felt a bit angry, 'Who exactly are you? And if you indeed are God then why the hell do you insist on coming to this forsaken tea shop!'

'Why, I like the tea.'

'A blatant lie! The tea here sucks, it's watery,' I looked at Ashok who was suddenly crestfallen, 'I am sorry, I mean the tea is quite good…never mind.'

He said softly, 'Look if it eases your mind, just assume what you want to assume about me…perhaps that method actor thing, yeah I am a method actor, I am shooting for a film, I am working in a play, believe what you will.' And then he left abruptly, like always.

For the next many weeks I always met him there and exchanged a few words. He never spoke anything profound, but always showed me some human interest story. I grew to look forward to his visits, perhaps he was slightly cranked, perhaps he had lost someone dear to him and this had affected him mentally making him believe that he was God. And if this was the case, who was I to break this illusion for him?

One day I asked him, 'If you are God, shouldn't you have to listen to over six billion prayers each day? Six billion screams, laments, even anyone who is happy with his life would have something to say to you. How do you deal with this?'

He looked pained when I asked him this, he tried to avoid the topic but I continued, 'You know the worst part of the day for you would be the morning, I mean even before you have properly woken up, millions of people are at your feet pouring milk on you, asking *hamaara ye Kaam karaa dijiye hamaara wo kaam kara dijiye*'

'Yes...that's true.'

'Then what does God...what do you do?'

He looked away and silently sipped tea, then he said 'I seriously don't want to talk about it.'

'Oh come on, you are God. How can you shy away from talking about something?'

'What do you humans do when you are faced with multiple tasks, multiple problems at the same time?' He asked me suddenly.

'Well I...I chose the problem that needs to be solved the most urgently and then I follow.'

'Now think of what would you do when you have six billion people telling you their problems simultaneously.'

I had no answer for this, I was about to light up my second cigarette when he said, 'I tune them. Like you would do to a radio, I shut a large number of these problems out.'

The cigarette fell from my hand; I said 'What do you mean you tune them? You mean to say that you shut out people who pray to you! How could you?' But then I realized that I had fallen under the assumption that he was actually God, so I calmed and said, 'No I meant...if God would do that, it would be awful.'

'I am not proud of it, okay...if I was able to listen to every scream, answer every prayer, help every good person in this world, then it would be a utopia. I cannot. I listen to them in phases, that way it is clearer, and I help as many people as I can. But I am not able to listen to all of them that is why these...these tragedies happen.'

In a weird way, what this man was saying made sense to me. If God ever needed an advocate, this man could be that person.

I never pestered him with questions about his Godliness after that. Instead I listened to his views on current affairs, and to his continuous stories of small but significant human achievements. He was very informed, and he had a nice way of telling things. Many times I wondered whether this man WAS actually God, trying to take a rest once in a while. I knew it was an implausible thing to think of, but then, there it was.

Then one day, everything went to hell.

I was coming to Hathua from a rather circuitous route because of construction work near Sigra, all traffic was in tatters, but then Banaras as a city had been perennially stuck in a traffic jam. I was standing in front of a traffic signal, and it started raining lightly. A small kid came to me and started wiping the fuel tank of my motorcycle, such kids can be seen at all traffic signals, looking for some money in exchange of cleaning up someone's car window, or someone's bike. I tried to shoo the kid away, but when he didn't go I took out a coin and asked the kid to go away. The kid started running away to the other side of the road in search of other vehicles. I was looking at something else when I heard the violent screech of rubber against asphalt. A lot of people screamed at the same time, and I saw couple of boys ride away on a motorcycle. I don't think anyone noted down their number.

When I turned to see where the screams came from, I saw something that I would never forget till the day I die. It was the kid...and he was...I...I don't think I can even write about it.

I felt frustrated, I was right there, I felt angry. I thought that I was the one who sent the kid to his death, I was the one who was responsible. No, I felt angry. I wanted those two boys to be punished, I wanted someone to blame. I wiped tears from my eyes and drove to Ashok's shop. I was going to give the God man a dose of bitter reality.

When I saw him he was sitting under the stairs drinking tea, oblivious of what I had witnessed. I didn't care that Ashok and his father were in hearing range, I snatched the paper away from him and said 'Do you know what I just saw! Do you know what...you....you call yourself God! You couldn't even save a little kid's life! And it happened just two kilometres away from you, and what did you do? Nothing!'

He was taken aback, he looked at me, as I started crying copiously, he got up and asked me to sit down in his place, 'Calm down friend...tell me what happened.'

Between sobs I told him what I had just seen, 'Please, please stop calling yourself God. You are no one, you are just like me, and you are powerless!'

He remained silent for a long time, having set his tea cup on a shelf near him. Then he spoke, 'I am sorry you had to witness that. But believe me, there was nothing that you could do. For my sake, do not blame yourself.'

'I blame you! So called God! Tell me, if you really are God, why didn't you...why didn't you do anything?'

He said, 'I told you, I cannot be at all the places at all time, do you think I would have allowed this...suffering around me...'

'Shut up! Shut up! Phoney idiot! You think, you still think all this is a Joke! You call yourself a God! Get away, away from my sight...*Ashok, Samjhao ise*...if I see him here again I will never ever come back to this place.'

Ashok had never seen me break down like this, he immediately left his cooking station and went to the man and said 'Please leave.'

The man said, 'No, not before I have had my say.'

Ashok was about to move forward when I saw him literally freeze in air. A quick glance around me showed that everything was a bit different, even the flame beneath the teapot seemed frozen, Sheetal and Ashok's father too looked like two-dimensional paintings. The man was standing in front of me, but his features seemed to be constantly changing, it was hard to say who or what he looked like. His voice came but it seemed devoid of a source, it was as if being fed directly to my ears.

'I have told you before, I will tell you again. Do you think I enjoy it when something of this sort happens?'

I was about to speak but realized that I could not.

'You saw one kid die and you are like this, think of me, a million maybe more of my children die every day. And I don't know how many more suffer injury, disease, heart ache, how many of them are constantly thinking of ending their lives. Do you think I allow this to happen out of choice? Blame God for everything, pray to God for everything. I am not all that your kind make out me to be! Yes, I have limitations, and yes I too feel the pain of loss! Do not tell me that I think of all this as a joke.

I come to this little shop, this place to escape it all. Yes! I shut out voices at times and I am not proud of it, but then there are millions that I do help. I am…I am still learning!

I am going from here, you don't believe that I am God, don't, it was better that way. But never for one second believe that I allow children to be butchered. It is not God that kills children, it is you! It is your kind! I am for all my powers most of the time trying to protect you from the harm that you cause yourselves!'

And suddenly there was an imploding flash and everything was back to the way it was. The man wasn't there anymore and Ashok was cleaning up his tea-shelf.

'Ashok, where's…where's that man?'

'Sir ji you told me to get rid of him, I did. He walked away, but Sir ji…let him come once in a while, he always gives one Re. extra…'

I was already on my way out to the market in search of him, I looked around, but he was so plain looking that in the crowded streets it was impossible to search for him. I searched for a while, then came back, mulling over what I had seen. Had it just been a product of the shock I was experiencing? I had no way to know.

Over the next few weeks I went to Ashok's shop in hope of meeting the man, but he was keeping up his end of the promise. I often thought why would God himself descend down to this tea shop? What did he stand to gain? What was it that he wanted to feel? I started to seek significance in his choice of tea shop, and I wondered if it was part of some bigger picture which I could not see at present. I knew I had to search for him, he had gone, he thought he had had his say but he had left a thousand things unanswered.

I grew restless. I started by doing what I now think is the most idiotic thing to have done, I googled for 'God Security Agency, Banaras' and then I looked for its variations, like 'Bhagwan Security Agency,' etc. I raked my brains for all the conversations that I had had with him, looking for any sort of detail that would tell me where he lived or what he did. Unfortunately it all came out to be blank.

I thought of starting to ask around, but I realized, he had never given me a name, even an alias. I couldn't very well go around hoping people would tell me where God lived. And then I went to the temples. Perhaps he would be there, perhaps he would wish to be actually physically present there when his devotees prayed to him. And in spite of myself I even prayed at Kashi Vishwanath.

One day I remembered that in the very beginning he had mentioned that some friend of his had told him about this shop at Hathua Market, and before that he went to Dashashwmedh ghat. On a Friday I decided to brave the Godowlia crowd and roamed around for hours on the ghat searching for him. Then I realized a fundamental mistake that I had been making. If I needed to search for a man (or God) who liked to visit a tea shop, I should start by looking at all the tea shops.

The stretch from Dashashwmedh to Assi Ghat is only a few kilometres and is quite walkable, so I started my search at Assi, looking at tea shops for him, especially at the smaller, obscure ones, and I always looked for someone reading a local newspaper.

For more than a month I cut time from work every Friday and searched at as many tea-shops as it was possible for me to do. Some of them started even noticing me, and on my repeat visits asked me brusquely what exactly was it that I wanted. I couldn't tell them, because I really didn't know. And describing him was not easy, he had the plain features of an everyman.

I was sure that I would not find him at any of the tea shops on the ghats, and I thought it would be impossible for me to look at every shop in the whole of Banaras, but a fool's hope and determination made me think that I could do it. But faced with the Herculean task at hand and the improbability of finding him again I broke down. I sat on the steps of Assi, pensive and distraught. I fished out my pack of cigarettes and smoked a couple of cigarettes when it was time for the *Aarti*. Out of reverence to the ritual I decided to stub out my cigarette and got up to leave the place when presently I saw a young girl standing in front of me.

'Here, look!' She was for some inexplicable reason waving a paper in front of me.

'What is it?' I asked while trying to focus on it.

'Oh, I am sorry, it is for a submission, and...well...my teacher doesn't think so but I think it's unethical without...'

175

'What are you talking about?' I was getting frustrated with her.

'Look! Look!' She handed me the paper. It was a rough outline for a pencil or charcoal sketch. And it was pretty much me, a man sitting on the steps with a cigarette in his hand and head bowed down in sadness. 'I will call it Sad Man with Cigarette...oops I mean, do you like it?'

I nodded a little and handed the paper back to her, hoping that this would make her go on her way, but she continued speaking 'Actually my friends...we are all from BHU...FOVA you know...anyway, they often come here, drawing sketches of people...speculating what their subjects...I mean people are thinking...I...I thought it better to ask...'

'What?'

'Mister...sir...why are you sad?'

I remained silent, having no wish to discuss things with a girl who had already invaded my privacy by sketching me without my permission.

'Please...you know...it would be helpful in class, to know the backstory...what happened?'

I moved away from her and started walking briskly but she started walking alongside me, I thought of pushing her, but then decided against it, she continued chattering non-stop, 'I won't even tell your name, I just want to know what happened'

I stopped and just to shut her up I half-shouted saying, 'I lost someone okay!'

She eyed me keenly and without a hint of sadness in her voice said, 'I am sorry to hear that. Who was she? Or he... I mean...a relative? Brother? Friend?'

'Friend...' I said.

'Oh that is very very sad…what happened…did he leave the city? Or something unfortunate happened, do you mind telling me…?'

But I was not listening to a word of what the girl was saying. Instead, what I had just said was playing inside my head.

And then, like a flash it came to my mind. All logic, everything about him coming down to that tea-shop became clear. In a moment I understood it all. I understood his reason, his motivation.

Friendship.

I smiled as I left the Ghat, I sped my motorcycle towards Ashok's shop and I was sure that the man/God would be there, I went with happiness warming me up. I was going to meet a friend.

THE BARBER STORY

It was a normal month of August for the city of Mumbai. It rained heavily, every alternate hour and all Mumbaikars waded through the pouring and stagnant water with practiced ease and discomfort. The sky was perpetually dark greyish, but the business of the city was as they say as usual.

In a less glamorous part of Colaba, which was the centre of the rich and famous South Bombay, far away from overpriced cafes and bars and yet within touching distance of the Gateway and the Taj was a small air-conditioned barber shop called London Hair Saloon. Barber shops in this part of the city had the tendency of naming themselves after Occidental cities, around the bend of the road which lead to the Radio Club was Rome Hair Dressers. Perhaps these names helped the foreign clientele identify with the shops easily (since Colaba has a sizeable floating *firangi* population). The owner and chief barber of London Hair Saloon was Mr Naseem Kidwai (formerly of Jaunpur) who was a tall and bulky man with a height much north of six feet. He was the best barber of south Bombay despite competing with organized trade of 'hair designers' who had opened salons quite near to his shop. A lot of ultra-rich Parsee gentlemen from

Cusrow Baug and those who lived in the high-rises of Cuffe Parade came down to this shop specifically to get their hair cut and beards shaved from Naseem.

And his fame and skill gave Naseem the power to choose his clients as per his will. He took appointments on phone and let the general public get tended to by his team of apprentice and learned barbers. However, Naseem was no snob, he would always go out of his way to service certain regular customers regardless of whether they would pay double the existing rate because getting a shave directly from Mr Naseem came at a premium cost.

Presently, Mr Naseem sat outside his shop on a plastic chair pulled against the wall next to his shop door and dully regarded the incessant rain. Out of force of habit he motioned with his hand and the boy at the small paan shop next to the South Indian restaurant across the road came running, dodging the medium-fast traffic easily. He knew that this was a call for the 'Khan Sahab's' cigarette break. He also knew that the Khan Sahib did not like to keep a packet with him because that would increase his intake of nicotine.

Naseem gave a Rs. 10 note for a stick that cost 8 and did not expect the boy to return him the small change. He took out his shiny silver Zippo lighter from his Kurta pocket and lit up the cigarette. For a while he smoked content with himself and enjoying the feeling of sitting just outside the border of the rain. He cherished the occasional droplet which landed on his feet or hand and the way the smoke that he exhaled disappeared into the torrent of rain.

It was the fourteenth of August, a day permanently etched into his memory. Twenty-five years ago this very day had made him the man he was right now, and he had made it a practice to write five hundred words every year in a small notebook which he always carried with him in his barber case. Presently he took out the notebook and admired his own calligraphic Urdu as he went over his past. Tomorrow was the auspicious day, and he would start writing again at midnight.

He had never wanted to be part of the family 'profession' (in eastern UP, there are no family businesses, just jobs that get passed on from generation to generation) and at the age of seventeen when his father wanted to pull him away from school he rebelled in a way his entire generation had been taught to rebel. He caught a train from Varanasi to Mumbai, travelling without ticket but with a pocketful of dreams. It was one of those off-season months (it was a time when off-season months existed) and he wasn't bothered by ticket collectors who let him lounge on a side-upper berth (which proved to be small for him even then) because he kept to himself and despite his towering frame he had a likeable baby face.

Naseem carefully chose to get down at three small stations to fill his bottle of water and eat the cheap but edible food of *Pooris* served with *aloo-gravy*. He had saved some money over the years by doing odd jobs for his carpenter uncle and also by collecting the Eidi he had received from his relatives time to time. He spent the money frugally, because films and cousins had told him that Mumbai was a very expensive place where a one-time meal was equal to an entire week's expense in Jaunpur.

After more than 28 hours of train travel he reached the Victoria Terminus station and was instantly overwhelmed by the huge station building, the stench of fish and the crowd of people who seemed to be in two minds on whether to enter this city or exit it.

He only had a small metal attaché case in way of luggage and he had crammed in two kurtas and one pair of pants, apart from this he carried only the small barber kit that his father had gifted to him on his 16th birthday, when he wanted to persuade him to start working at his shop. Inside the kit apart from his regular shaving instruments he had a small notebook and a black and white photograph of home.

Once outside the station he was awed to see how solid all the buildings seemed, they were tall imposing structures made out of giant bricks and all of them had the same official type colour of muddy brown. A cousin had told him that all these buildings had been built by British because they mirrored the architecture of England and it made them feel at home. His cousin had found it all quite ugly but Naseem at present was in awe of what he saw. It had been less than an hour since he had alighted from the train and already he was half in love.

It was at this exact moment when he was looking at the buildings which surrounded him presently that a man collided with him, muttered a hasty apology and started running again. Running after him at some distance was another man who suddenly shouted 'Stop him! Stop the thief!'

By this time there was a gap between the man being chased and Naseem, and to this day he does not know what powered him but he threw the metal attaché that he was carrying and it expertly hit the fleeing man on the back of his head. He stumbled and fell on the pavement next to hawkers selling plastic sunglasses, as the crowd gave way to the falling man. His attaché flew open and his sparse luggage stumbled out. Naseem quickly ran after his clothes while the man who was giving chase caught up with the sprawled man on the pavement and landed a vicious punch on his face.

Naseem looked ruefully at his soiled clothes and stuffed them back in his attaché; he got up to see the man he had helped catch a thief walking towards him. In his hand was a thick purse which bulged with currency notes. The man held out his hand towards Naseem and said 'Thank you kid. Keep this, it will help you wash your clothes.' And before Naseem knew, there was a crisp Rs. 100 note in his hand.

This cumulative event, from hitting that man with a flying attaché to getting a currency denomination in his hand which he hadn't seen in his life was what set the course for the rest of Naseem's life. While he looked at the note in disbelief the man had already disappeared into the crowd, there was a fat police constable accosting the thief at a distance, and Naseem knew that it would be better if he didn't hang around long enough for the policeman to ask him questions.

Later when he was sitting on a cot in a tiny room inside a dilapidated building in Byculla, he remembered making a note in his book *'The City is Big On the Outside and Very Small on The Inside'*. The size of the room had worried him, it was like living inside a matchbox. And at least for the next month or so he had to share it with a friend who had actually been generous enough to let him cohabit for some time.

The building was huge but the ceiling was low, and Naseem with his tall frame felt like he was forever at risk of banging his head against the roof. The room had a cot, an old mattress and two stools along with a small table fan. He knew that this was going to take some getting used to, his father was not a rich man, and still they had their own house with a small garden and a courtyard in Jaunpur.

It was very hard for him to ward off disillusionment, during his initial days he kept telling himself that this is the place where people come to get their dreams fulfilled. This was the city of Amitabh Bachchan and the Tatas. All he needed to do was find a Naseem-shaped hole and he would fit right in.

Unfortunately, he hadn't really thought through about what he wanted to do after coming to Bombay. His friend, the one whose money-sending back home capabilities were his main motivation to leave everything and come to this city was at the end of the day doing what Naseem had wanted to escape in the first place. He had told everyone at Jaunpur that he was headwaiter at a decent restaurant in a posh locality. He was actually a barber in a normal barber shop in Byculla. The money was steady and it was a fulltime job, but it wasn't what had dragged Naseem here.

He tried getting any and all jobs possible. One of his initial jobs was that of a helper at a clothes shop in Grant road, and he tried to supplement his income by working as a part-time waiter at the many restaurants in that area. But he wasn't able to hold on to any one job for a long time. One of the reasons for this was that his imposing personality often made the original *Seths* feel dwarfed. A shop-boy is supposed to be meek and small, he shouldn't look like the de facto owner of the shop. And even in a city with a general disdain for human life, a man's ego was a big thing.

For the first year Naseem wasn't able to hold on to any one particular job for more than four weeks at a time, however, even with these temporary jobs he was able to earn more money than he could have as a barber in his home town. And after he sent the first money order home, his parents too reconciled with his decision to live in Bombay.

After the first two months his friend was happy to accept a rent for subletting the mattress on his floor, and thus Naseem had a six feet by four feet area which he could call his since he paid a monthly fees for it. Both of them worked long hours in their jobs, trying to scrape as much money as possible, and the one off day that they got in the week did not clash. Thus, they lead separate life styles in which they hardly met or talked to each other, as a result, they got along rather well.

Life had set itself in a rhythm with his string of semi-permanent jobs and a more or less steady income. Naseem had not really achieved what he wanted to when he came to Bombay, but on the other hand he didn't really know what it was that he had wanted to achieve in the first place. For an entire year he took things as they came, not mulling too deeply on where his life was heading.

And then one day his friend fell sick. It was perhaps something to do with the month of August and the incessant rains. He caught a fever which showed no signs of abating. For a week he could hardly stand up, the fever weakened him and kept him bed ridden. Naseem stayed home the entire time taking care of his friend. And since both of them had jobs which paid them daily wages, their incomes suddenly stopped.

He had earned a lot more than Naseem and would more often than not pay out more in their day to day expenses. And so between them they decided that it was more important for them to save his job. He said 'There is no dearth of people looking for a job; I don't know till how long will the *Seth* keep my position vacant. He has a busy shop and cannot spare a single man. Naseem, I want you to work there until I get better.' Naseem knew that he would have to do the very thing that he had rebelled against at home, but at present it was either that, or to cope up with homelessness and starvation in Bombay.

'But what is the guarantee that the *Seth* will accept me in your stead? Why would he trust me with his customers?'

His friend laughed lightly and said, 'As long as you do not cut someone's throat it would be okay. And besides, the *Seth* is a *bhaiyya*, like us. He has a soft corner for *bhaiyyas*. Tell him about your barber shop in Jaunpur, and also that you are a fourth generation barber, *hajamat* is in your blood. This would be enough to convince him. Besides, it is only a matter of a week or so.'

The next day Naseem found himself on a bus from Byculla to Nagpada. The area was like a small city within a very big metro. The rain amplified the smells of stale chicken feathers and old oil, and the streets looked like they leaked tar upwards. Naseem cursed the rains and state of the place and searched for

'New Broadway Hair Dressers'. The shop was in one of the by-lanes from the main road leading to Saat Rasta, but it was huge. The size of the shop reminded him of his primary school, and his first reaction was to get intimidated.

The *Seth* sat behind a table at the far end of the room, exactly the way a teacher would sit. And he regarded Naseem and his barber case keenly. 'Yes?' He barked loudly, 'What do you want?' He had an eye for identifying potential customers and time wasters. And this tall young man seemed to belong to the second category.

Naseem went to the table and bowed slightly, '*Salaam* sahib. I am Bilal's friend. My name is Naseem and I come from Jaunpur. I have come here to work.'

'Work? Work! Where the hell is that rascal Bilal? He doesn't come to work for an entire week and now he suddenly sends another *gaonwalla* of his for a job here? Does he think I have a job factory here? Go, whatsyourname, I don't have a job for you.'

Naseem bowed again and said, 'I beg your pardon sir. I have not come here for a job. Bilal has been unwell for a week and he wants to ensure that during his absence your shop work does not suffer.'

'What? If he is unwell he will send any *aira gaira* to work on his behalf? Does he think I am running a *wakda* here? Go back and tell Bilal that either he joins tomorrow or his job is gone too.'

Naseem kept his barber case quietly on the table and opened it. He took out the straight razor and presented it to the *Seth*, 'Sir, I am from a family of barbers. I have a shop which is famous in the whole of Jaunpur, and I am sure that I will not give you cause for dissatisfaction.'

The *Seth* snatched the straight razor from his hand and examined it closely, 'No plastic handle, it has a certain shine to it...I like it that it is one of the old *ustarahs*.' He took a deep breath and pulled the barber case towards him and went though it with his grubby fingers. 'What's your name?'

'Naseem Kidwai.'

'Naseem, Bilal is a good worker here. There are customers who like him a lot. He brings me a lot of good business. But, I can remove him with a click of my fingers. And I might as well as do it.'

He waited for Naseem to respond, but the kid stood in front of him, looking at him impassively. He continued, 'I am going to give you a chance. Only one chance. You will be here for a week. You will not be paid, but I will give you lunch. One plate *Misal Pav* daily. After a week if Bilal comes back he can have his job back. But even after this if he doesn't come back or you make a mistake, it will be the end of his job.'

Naseem said nothing. He nodded once but betrayed no reaction at all.

The *seth* sighed. 'You start this instant. And you will work for a ten hour shift. Maqsood, tell him where things are. Now go! I want to see work!'

As it turned out there was no other threat to Bilal's job apart from his own ill health. Naseem was a better than average barber. He literally had *hajamat* in his blood. So when Bilal had to extend his sick leave to an entire month because he was too weak to come back to work and his fever didn't leave him for more than twenty days, the *Seth* grudgingly let Naseem continue. He also started paying him an apprentice's salary, he clearly stated that he did not deserve Bilal's salary as of now. Naseem did not complain, what he was getting paid here was more than what he got at his odd jobs, and now at least there was a flow of income. The Seth had agreed to give a small advance salary for Bilal's medical expenses. This additional money tided Naseem and

Bilal through the sickness until he was well enough to start work again.

By the time Bilal finally came back to work Naseem had been well entrenched, albeit as a newcomer, in the barber shop. The *Seth* had decided to keep him for at least six months more because Naseem had a certain finesse as a barber, and the *Seth* had to pay him much lesser than experienced barbers even though he was better than many of them. The *Seth* kept him on as a low cost future replacement of the first guy to leave.

It had now been a year since Naseem had first stepped inside the barber shop with his plea and razor pack. He had attracted a coterie of familiar clients. Like in his previous jobs here too he stood out because of his tall lanky frame. This distinguished him from the other barbers with their weather-beaten darkened skin and diminutive statures. And he had picked out his expertise, channelling his own love of films he had become an expert on filmy hair styles. It was tricky because it involved giving shape to long hair and ensuring it does not become too short. And the *Seth* was happy because styling involved a premium. So in effect he was earning more from Naseem by paying him less.

Naseem too had more or less accepted that being a barber was ultimately part of his destiny. He had been a natural at his job and the effortlessness of it all took him from day to day without his profession becoming a burden on him. He was spared the shifting of a job every other month or so and with the steady money his life in this city had become more comfortable.

There are two kind of barbers, those who stay completely silent and thus compel their clients to chatter, or those who find a way to keep on talking while they work. Naseem and his ilk were of the former type. They did their work silently and diligently, allowing their clientele to be talkative. And there was a particular set of clients who talked a lot.

Naseem was no simpleton and over a period of time he could discern that there was a certain segment of customers who had a habit of bumping into each other at his shop on the third or fourth Sunday of every month. They would talk in a rhythmic pattern of code words. Through them Naseem got to know that unwittingly he had been living and working close to the nerve centre of the change in the structure of Bombay's criminal class. His knowledge till now on that topic had both been aided by and limited to films like Deewar and Shaan. He viewed gangsters as mythical beings who lived public lives in palatial sea side houses and had an army of bodyguards at their beck and call. The criminals who talked of large sums in front of him did not fit any filmy description. They were all quite average looking and except for a few of them mostly they wore average looking clothing. The middle aged ones spoke with reverence of the time gone by and of the adventures they had had at the Mazgaon dock, they also spoke with disdain for the new kid who had ousted the old *Maaliks* and was trying to change the rules of the game. However, most of the younger crowd spoke in awe of the new Don and they always used the honorific *Bhai* for him.

This new Don had a house in one of the busiest and most congested areas of Mumbai. This new Don whose name the city had learnt in the past four years had a fortress in Naupada. And right now the shift in the Underworld's order was at its peak. This man was the constant topic of keen discussion amongst this particular set of customers, some of them even subtly claimed to work for him.

Then one fine day into the shop walked the man whose wallet Naseem had helped save on his first day in the city. He was dressed sharply and walked with a swagger. When *Seth* saw him he got up in a hurry and greeted him. They exchanged pleasantries and he then asked one of his shop boys to tell the Nagori shop next door to make his best tea possible. The man meanwhile sat down on one of the waiting chairs and took out a pack of expensive looking cigarettes. When the tea came he offered one to *Seth* and lit one up himself.

The *Seth* asked him politely that how come his *Eid ka Chand* had shown itself after two years. The man smiled and hissed smoke through the corners of his upturned lips. He looked around conspiratorially and asked *Seth* to bring his ear closer to him. But instead of whispering he loudly spoke the name of a city. Dubai.

Then he started talking freely about his days in Dubai, about the grandeur of the Sheikhs and about the future and about how Dinars are now more coveted than Dollars. He held out a crisp Dinar in front of him and then clasped it into the *Seth*'s hand in a similar fashion to which he had given Naseem the hundred rupee note.

Till then he had not noticed Naseem in the shop. When he finally saw him he displayed only a flicker of recognition. But Naseem recognized him immediately. It was more so because of the incident at VT than with how the man looked.

On an impulse during a lull in the conversation between the *Seth* and the man he stepped up and said, 'Sir, do you remember me?'

The man squinted his eyes and replied, 'Not really young man. I might have seen you somewhere but in Bombay it is impossible to remember everyone you see.'

'Sir once I helped you catch a thief at VT around two years back. He was running away with your purse.'

The man smiled, 'Yes...I think I remember. You had thrown your luggage at him. It was a solid throw! You helped me save quite a lot of money. Did I give you a reward that day?'

'Yes sir. You gave me some money to wash my clothes which had become dirty.'

The man's smile turned into a chuckle, 'What a coincidence,' he said, 'And what are you doing here in Pasha Bhai's shop?'

The *Seth* intervened, 'He...a...he works here. He's one of my barbers.'

'*Behtareen*, so why not trim my beard today? I haven't really had a chance to keep it in order for some time. Young man, are you a good barber?'

'*Arre* sir why do you want the boy to attend to you, you are a treasured friend, I will myself give you a trim.'

'Pasha Bhai, I will not have you troubled. You have so many good lads, why not let this young man have a go at me.'

The *Seth* paled visibly and a film of sweat started forming on his forehead. He went to Naseem and whispered, 'You will have to be very careful, this man is not your *gully ka chhokra* crowd who wants a filmy style cut. This is a very important and powerful man, and if he is dissatisfied after getting up from that chair, I will cut your throat off with your own *ustarah*.'

Naseem nodded and cleaned one of the wooden chairs vigorously with his shop cloth. He politely gestured towards the chair and asked the man to sit. The man stubbed out his cigarette in his tea glass and with a small hop got up to sit on the chair.

The man kept talking throughout the time Naseem attended to him, making it difficult for Naseem to properly give a shape to his beard. Pasha Bhai, with whom he was conversing, kept his answers short and succinct, in the hope that it will stop the man from speaking so much. Naseem decided to be slow and careful, and in the end when the man got up from the chair, he stroked his beard and said, '*Masha Allah,* you have cut it like a gardener mows a rich man's lawn! Solid!'

Naseem bowed and said, 'It would be 8 ana sir.'

The man looked at him and then at Pasha Bhai, who had by then turned a ghostly white, he laughed a throaty laugh and said, 'Young lad, I don't carry such small change with me.'

The man then turned towards Pasha Bhai and bade a quick farewell, post which he walked out from the shop. As soon as the two swinging doors came to a standstill, Pasha Bhai who must have been holding his breath for at least ten minutes, exhaled.

'*Ya Allah, Barkhurdar!* DO YOU HAVE ANY IDEA WHO YOU WERE TALKING TO?'

Naseem, in all honesty, said that he didn't.

Pasha Bhai picked up a newspaper from his table and waved it in front of him, brandishing it like a sword, 'Dimwit, do you read this thing?'

Naseem again replied earnestly that he did not read newspapers.

Pasha Bhai fished out a two pager from within and pointed out towards a small news print, 'Read this! Have you heard of this man? TELL ME YOU GAONWALLAH HAVE YOU HEARD OF THIS MAN?'

The photograph was black and white, it was of a man wearing a coat and a bow tie, a clean shaven man who had sunglasses on. The name below the photograph was one he had heard a few times in a shop, always with an honorific 'Bhai' attached after it, and by now he had begun to recognize the difference between a colloquial Bhai and an honorific Bhai.

Naseem pointed out that this was not the man who had come to the shop.

'Of course not you idiot. This man will never step inside such a small shop as mine. The man who came in is the right hand of this man. Do you know who you asked 8 ana from? Do you have any idea?

This time Naseem stayed silent and shifted his gaze away.

Pasha Bhai sighed, went back to his desk and lit a *beedi*, 'The man that you shaved today is Hasan Murtuza. A wanted smuggler. A man against whom the police try as far as possible to not file a case because of the name connected to him. This is one man you should distance yourself from. Do you know why?'

Naseem shook his head in a no.

'Because Hasan Murtuza is the right-hand man of Shakir Ilyas Kaskar!'

The full import of what Pasha Bhai had said that day did not hit Naseem until in the night aided by the sleepy rumblings of his friend about what a big and powerful man Shakir Ilyas was and how Hasan Murtuza was the most dangerous man he had seen with naked eyes, along with what he had heard over the time period about the shift in the underworld of Mumbai he finally understood at least partly about the man he had dealt with today.

The next morning when he walked into work he fully expected the Seth to issue marching orders to him. Instead he saw Pasha Bhai sitting with his hands crossed smiling benevolently. On the table was a shiny tin of 555 cigarettes. Pasha called Naseem and opened the tin, offering him a cigarette. When Naseem declined politely he said, 'When your *Seth* offers you a cigarette, you smoke a cigarette.'

It turned out that Hasan Murtuza had been mildly amused by the naivety of the gaonwallah from UP and he was wholly pleased with his trim. He had called Pasha Bhai to his house the night before to give him his gift from Dubai. And Pasha Bhai at present breathed easy, letting out twin cones of smoke from the corner of his lips.

One month later on a slow morning when Naseem came back from his first tea break he saw Pasha Bhai pacing restlessly across the room. He stopped short when he saw Naseem and gestured urgently with his hand to call him, 'This is very weird.' He said, 'It is a strange request, I haven't heard anything of this sort happening for the past couple of years.'

He touched his shoulder lightly and strode out of the shop next to the paan *gumti* next door. He lit up a cigarette nervously and offered another to Naseem, who by now knew better than to refuse. He continued being cryptic, 'These are dangerous people. I can mingle with them because I am old and who cares, but...'

Naseem was in the habit of not interrupting his *Seth* when he went on one of his monologues, he decided that this was not a good time to break that habit and his silence ensured that the *Seth* carried on speaking after a pause.

'I am going to send one guy with you. Not with you but after you. He will remain hidden in the PCO shop in front of his house. If there is a problem you shout, he will phone from there and I will come...we all will come.'

When Pasha Bhai had finished his first cigarette he quickly lit another one and unwittingly exhaled smoke on Naseem's face. 'Kid. Hasan Murtuza has called you over to his house for a haircut. I don't want you to go but I don't want to refuse him either. So go. I will make sure that you are safe. This I promise, *Insha-Allah.*'

For all the talk of Dubai and Dinars, Hasan Murtuza lived in a two room house with room sizes not particularly bigger than what Naseem's own rooms in the chawl were. This he learnt over the course of time was for anonymity. It was very hard for someone who did not know the exact house to look for him in the building that he lived in, all doors were like in the city of Alibaba and Chalis Chor, but since there was no Marjini to mark them, Hasan lived safely.

'Keep it neat,' he said, as he sat on a wooden chair in front of an almirah whose right door served as a mirror. 'Nothing too filmy, no style, but neat and clean. See how simple but good Bhai's style is.'

Naseem nodded and got to work, his scissors working their magic on the mass of unclean and unruly hair on top of Murtuza's head. After half an hour when the metal stopped clicking and swishing and Naseem removed the waste hair from Murtuza's person, the reflection on the almirah smiled devilishly, '*Bahut khoob*. Tell Pasha Bhai that I am happy. And you would come here every month to do this for me.'

That night he came back to Byculla and wrote a single page detailing the day's events, starting with the line *I have cut the devil's hair today. A charade which I hope I will not have to maintain much longer.*

Against his will and better judgement these monthly visits became a regular fixture, and because of Naseem's propensity to listen more and speak less, the devil spoke freely. Soon, to brag off in front of the *gaonwala* he started detailing his crimes. The wallet that Naseem had saved from getting stolen on his first day most probably contained stolen money, or money earned by doing an unholy deed. Hasan was an important man for the new crime king of Mumbai, even though he did not look the part. While he himself stayed in a non-descript place he told Naseem glamorous tales of sea facing bungalows, and parties that start after midnight because of the Bhai's insistence. He talked about the rich and powerful cowering in fear, and about beautiful people getting smitten by the power that Bhai and his men wield.

'The future, *Insha-Allah*, is ours.' Hasan would say, between puffs of smoke.

There was a telephone in Hasan's room, an old style device with an intricate cradle and receiver. Naseem had been coming to Hasan's house for six months now and had never once heard the phone ringing. And yet from time to time he could see

Hasan looking at the phone nervously, anxiously hoping for it to simultaneously ring and not ring. Naseem had once asked Hasan politely whether he could share the number of this phone with Pasha Bhai, so that in case of emergency Naseem could be contacted. Hasan had laughed it off, saying that only one man in the entire world had this number.

On the seventh visit the phone rang, Hasan was in the middle of having his hair cut but he literally jumped from his chair to grab it. 'Assalam *Waleikum Bhai, Ji...ji Bhai*' He quickly motioned Naseem to go out of his room, and then he closed the door behind him.

Naseem could hear a muffled version of Hasan's end of the conversation, it was mostly quiet from his side except for punctuations of *Ji Bhai* every now and then. After around ten minutes the door opened and Hasan called Naseem back inside. It was funny to see that this devil of a man was sweating profusely.

He told Naseem to sit on the cot next to his chair. He then opened a drawer and took out a revolver, he pointed it towards Naseem and said, 'I can kill you.'

It was Naseem's turn to sweat, he tried all measures of self-control and still panic crept into his voice, 'What...what happened sir?'

'Nothing. But always remember that if I want, I can kill you. One shot. *Khallaas.*' He put the gun back in the drawer and said, 'The building people fear me, if someone hears the shot and asks what everyone will say is that I have a habit of shooting at birds.'

'But...but what have I done sir, is the haircut bad?'

'Forget the haircut.' Hasan said, 'I want you to do something for me. And if you tell anyone about it you will be dead. Remember that.'

Naseem nodded. He would remember that.

'Come, barber-boy, today is your lucky day.'

Naseem followed Hasan who had in actuality forgotten about his haircut, he had quickly worn a shirt over his singlet and rushed down his building to a derelict garage next to it. There was a total of three cars parked, one of them a blue ambassador. Hasan got inside the ambassador and told Naseem to do likewise.

Hasan drove as furiously as the traffic allowed him to, he cursed frequently and fought against the cluttered traffic of Byculla on his way across the Mohd Ali road. Bombay however did not give way for Hasan Murtaza.

After an agonizing drive of more than half an hour in stifling humidity and the Bombay sun while listening to the constant cursing of Hasan Murtaza, the car stopped in front of a blue coloured building at a relatively less crowded road near Masjud Bunder. 'Follow me quickly.' He said. He ran up three flights of stairs and knocked on the second door in the corridor. He knocked lightly at first, but after waiting for some time with no answer he called up Naseem. 'When I say, kick.'

Naseem was dumbfounded. 'Sir..?'

Hasan caught him by the collar, 'Don't sir me. When I say kick, you kick. Do you understand?'

Naseem nodded slightly.

They stood side by side in front of the door. Naseem waited, when he heard Hasan say 'Now' he kicked with all his energy. Hasan too kicked. The door cracked at the lock and jerked open. Hasan ran inside the room lightning fast and Naseem followed cautiously. Inside the room a young boy was sitting cowered on a bed. Hasan grabbed the boy by the neck and slapped him. He turned to Naseem, 'Put the door back in its place and jam it with that chair.' Naseem did as he was told, he could hear Hasan slapping the boy.

'Bastard. Look at me, look at me you bloody bastard.' Hasan tried to lift the boy's face. Naseem flinched as Hasan slapped him again.

'Give me your gun. Give me your damn gun.' Hasan started pat-searching the boy. The boy meekly pointed towards the pillow. Hasan removed a gun from there and put it in front of the boy's face, 'This is trouble, you understand?'

He got up and pocketed the gun, 'What do I do? What do I do with you young man!'

He turned to Naseem, 'What should we do with this bastard, barber-boy?'

Naseem couldn't even shrug. Hasan continued, 'I will tell you what we will do. You hold this idiot's hands.' The boy started crying silently, and Naseem in a trance went behind the boy and locked his hands within his own. Hasan took the gun and hit the boy on his knees with the butt viciously. The boy let out a huge shout, 'Don't shout you ass. Don't shout or I will put a bullet in your throat! Naseem see that he doesn't shout. Naseem!'

Involuntarily Naseem's hand moved to shut the boy's mouth. Hasan worked the boy's knees for a while and said, 'This will keep you out of trouble for some time. Now sleep you bastard!' And he landed an immense blow on the boy's forehead, making him unconscious.

'*Utha, utha saale ko*'. Hasan carried the boy with one hand across his shoulder and the other across Naseem's. They dragged the boy downstairs and kept him in the backseat of the ambassador. 'Get in'.

Naseem got in again and Hasan started driving, manoeuvring the car away from the crowded roads until they came across the broader highway which lead to the northern part of the city. The streets were much broader than what Naseem had been used to. In the nearly two years that he had spent in the metropolitan he had not gone beyond Dadar, and even then he had used the suburban train network. Now Hasan was speeding fast on the road, and soon they crossed Dadar. Hasan seemed to be in a better mood now, with one hand on the steering wheel he took out an audio cassette of the movie Karz from the glove compartment and started playing music in the car. He sang along with Kishore Kumar as he drove recklessly, occasionally glancing at his watch.

After two songs he stopped the player and asked Naseem, 'Do you want to know what all this is about?'

Naseem knew better than to say yes. He shook his head quickly in the negative.

'This...this bastard here is too young to even tie his shoes properly. But he wanted to become a hero, he thinks he is Agent Vinod or someone. He tried to directly attack someone from the Surve gang. And he killed some unknown *tapori* instead.'

Naseem wanted to ask that in the sea of crimes that his gang or these gangs commit, how it mattered that some poor *tapori* was killed. His silence brought him the answer.

'That *tapori* was the son of a Police constable, a constable who had once been a junior to Bhai's father. And now Bhai has asked me to take care of this...' Hasan stopped speaking, perhaps realizing that either he was revealing too much or that he needed to concentrate on the road.

Naseem was keeping an eye on the shops and hotels that lined the road to know where he was in. He had heard the names of all these places. They crossed Matunga, Sion and then Hasan took a turn towards Chembur. Naseem wanted to know who this kid was and why was he important enough for Hasan to directly deal with him. He mustered courage and asked, 'Hasan Bhai, who is this kid?'

Hasan cursed and spat and said, 'He is someone who is only alive because Bhai has given his word to his *mooh bolii* sister Inayat Bibi that no harm will come to him. You see, Bhai is generous. And this idiot is the kid of Inayat Bibi who wants to become the next Don before the dawn of tomorrow morning.'

Hasan moved his car expertly through well-chosen roads and he crossed Chembur and headed towards New Bombay. At one particular turn he moved away from the main road and on to a narrow path that went through a small patch of trees and lead towards a vast green field. In the middle of the field was a small house with an asbestos roof, Hasan stopped the car in front of the house and knocked violently on the door. A vicious man with a gigantic beard opened the door with anger in his eyes but cowed instantly as he saw Hasan.

'Hasan Bhai...something serious? You could have called me...I would have come to Dongri...'

'Altaf this is something so serious that I left my hair-cut in between. Look I even brought my barber with me.' Hasan pointed at Naseem and laughed lightly. He beckoned Naseem, who had not got out of the car because he didn't know whether he was supposed to or not, and when he came he asked him to go with Altaf and bring the boy out of the car. Altaf and Naseem carried the boy inside the house.

'Take care of this boy for one month. He is the son of our Bhai's Aapa, and he needs to stay out of trouble. Hurt his legs but don't break any bones. Slap him around but don't leave a mark. He is young and foolish and needs to be out of the limelight for some time. If something happens to him I will cut your head off and feed it to crows.' Hasan said this as a matter of fact and then along with Naseem he quickly left the scene.

That day without officially joining his organization Naseem moved one step closer to Hasan Murtaza. And he hated himself for it. He had helped Hasan hide a perpetrator of a crime and had also helped him commit a crime of sorts himself. Plus Hasan had threatened him with death if he chose to talk about it. It was a frustrating day for Naseem.

He bided his time patiently and worked diligently on his monthly visits to Murtuza. There was only one other instance in which he had to help his client by delivering a stack of oily guns wrapped in a cloth to a shady rich man living on Pedder Road. Apart from that all his other visits were strictly restricted to Hasan getting a haircut or a trim of the beard.

Seven months after the day Naseem had helped Hasan hide that boy he decided to ask Hasan a favour.

'Sir, I hope I have been a loyal and proficient barber to you.'

Hasan was surprised by this sudden declaration by his barber-boy and he quickly nodded in affirmative. 'Yes, so?'

'And I believe you are always satisfied with the haircut or the trim.'

'Come to the point lad. What is it? What has happened, are you going away somewhere?'

Naseem paused for around thirty seconds, he had rehearsed the simple one line request many times in his head and he wanted to say it perfectly.

'I want you to introduce me to Shakir Bhai.'

Hasan smiled, amused once again by the audacity of the greenhorn standing in front of him and also by the politeness and yet absurd nature of this request. He had in the past entertained this request from politicians, union workers and tangentially for a couple of actors. Today his barber wanted to meet up Bhai.

'Are you crazy? What will I tell Bhai? My barber wants to meet you? Sounds ridiculous.'

'Sir, I have heard that Bhai is generous....'

'You must be confusing Shakir bhai with Haji sahib or Vardabhai. Yes, Bhai is generous, but doesn't mean he will hold court for any *aira-gaira-natthu-khaira.*'

Naseem was ready for this reply. With a childlike smile he said, 'But sir, I am not an aira-gaira, I am the personal barber for Mr Hasan Murtuza.'

Hearing this Hasan Murtuza started laughing his throaty laugh once again. He was chuffed to bits with the obvious flattery by this lowly barber, and once again he caught himself admiring the cheek of the blighter standing in front of him. He wiped a small tear from his eye that had come with the laughter and asked him again, 'No but seriously, why do you want to meet Bhai? He is not a film star that you would ask for an autograph nor is he a tourist attraction that you want to take a photograph with him. Bhai does not have time to waste because of the businesses he runs. Now tell me, why exactly do you want to meet him?'

'I have no business to offer to Bhai. I am not that big. And yet I have heard so much about Bhai from you and from other people in this area that I am certain there is a particular matter in which only Shakir bhai can help me. Please, accept this one request of mine. You know I have never asked for anything else.'

Hasan eyed him keenly, 'What is this matter that you speak of? And why haven't you talked to me regarding this? Do you think Hasan Murtuza would not be able to help you?'

Naseem grinned weakly and said, 'Sir for almost all matters under Allah's benign sun I wouldn't need to think of anything but to turn towards you for help. But this is a very personal matter and I really need to see Bhai regarding this.'

Hasan said, 'Let me think of this for a while. I highly doubt whether Bhai will agree. Remind me two weeks from now.'

Although he did not come through with his demand two weeks later, in fact Hasan disappeared for more than a month. Naseem would dutifully go to his house to check up on him and instead would see an Aligarhi lock hanging on the door. Word on the street was that he had gone back to Dubai for six months.

However, he returned much before six months and when he saw Naseem again he said, 'Yes yes, I remember what you wanted. Be patient, the stars are on your side. The past one month has been very profitable for us. Bhai is in a good mood, I will persuade him to give you five minutes of his time some weeks from now.'

Naseem was satisfied with this. He had taught himself an immense amount of patience to ward-off the pace of the city from getting to him. He could easily wait a fortnight more without feeling any qualms about the same.

It turned out that within two weeks of this conversation Hasan called up Pasha bhai's shop on an off-day from his regular schedule and instructed Naseem to directly meet him near the movie theatre at Saat Rasta at three in the afternoon. Naseem asked permission for leaving early since he had to do some preparation before meeting the Don. He changed into a fresh shirt, packed his personal Barber-kit and then took a bus to Saat Rasta.

Today Hasan had come in a grey coloured Fiat. He was sweating profusely in the Bombay heat and he told Naseem to get in quickly. 'This is a bad idea.' He said, 'If Bhai gets angry I am going to have your head.' He kept on grumbling for some time. Naseem was surprised to see that they weren't going to Pakmodia Street where the Don was supposed to have his huge house. Instead they were now in front of the Mahalaxmi station and were heading towards Tulsi Pipe Road. As if reading his mind, Hasan said, 'What? You seriously thought I would take you to the Don's house? Do you think I am that crazy?'

Naseem remained his stoic self and did not speak a word during the journey. He instead concentrated on the road and the surroundings. This was the Western side of the city, there was a steady breeze coming from the sea which calmed his nerves. He was going to meet a man who inspired fear in the city, and he wanted to remain fearless.

They stopped at a white house near the sea in Bandra. It was a small house with a metal gate big enough for a car to go through, there were two guards in plain clothes standing on either side of the gate, their pistols jutting out of holsters attached to their belts. They gave a crisp nod to Hasan as he got out of the car and almost simultaneously greeted him with 'Salaam Hasan Bhai.' Hasan tossed the key to the car of one of them and told him to park it somewhere safe. Naseem followed Hasan and the guards presumed that this was one of Hasan's guests.

Inside the gate Naseem surveyed the house. It had two floors, both the floors had huge tinted windows on the side towards the sea, there was no balcony, and the main door was a simple wooden affair. Hasan knocked thrice and then pushed the door open. There was one more guard standing near the door on the inside who quickly saluted Hasan and then guided the way in. There were three rooms on the ground floor, one which seemed to operate as a kitchen, a larger room which was like a waiting area. There was a young woman wearing a short dress who was in the waiting area, she was lazily flipping through pages of a filmy magazine. Hasan told him to wait there and he quickly entered the third room.

Naseem counted the seconds to pass the time, neither he nor the woman tried to initiate conversation. The third person in the room---the guard did not pay any attention to him. He concentrated on the sounds that he heard, apart from the occasional sound of glossy paper being turned, the constant whirring of the ceiling fan and a low hum of the air-conditioning he could hear nothing at all. He surmised that the third room was completely sound proof. This he was sure was done to keep the Don's dealings secret even from his close bodyguards.

After more than half an hour in which he observed the guard still absolutely still and the young woman go through three filmy magazines the door opened and Hasan stuck his head out. 'You!' He said brusquely, 'Come inside quickly.'

It was supposed to be a big moment in Naseem's life, through a chance encounter at a railway station he had got acquainted with Hasan Murtuza, because of a random illness which his friend suffered he had got a job in barbershop and it had finally lead to him meeting the most dreaded man in the city right now. He felt a slight rush of fear, and then suppressed it. He pushed open the door and went inside.

Ultimately it turned out to be an anti-climax. The man in front of him was hardly thirty years of age, he did not look menacing, nor did he look like a flashy movie villain. He looked like a successful businessman with the only distinguishing factor being his droopy moustache. Hasan went and stood next to him, there were three empty chairs for Naseem to choose from and yet he remained standing, knowing well that it would be a folly to sit before being asked to.

He wasn't asked to sit, instead Hasan gave a very short introduction, 'Bhai, this is Naseem. He helped me take care of Inayat Bibi's son. He has been wanting to meet you for quite some time. Isn't it right Naseem?'

He nodded, and then spoke, 'Bhai, I have heard your praises not just in Byculla and Naupada but across the city. People would give their right arm to meet you, and I consider myself fortunate, I am thankful to you as well as to Hasan Bhai for giving me this chance.'

The Don nodded slightly and motioned with his hand, asking him to speak further.

'Sir I am a lowly barber, but I come from a family of traditional barbers. Bombay has given me a chance to work, this is a city of dreams and I am very sure that this city will help me fulfil my dreams. The key to the city is however in your hands, and so I know that for my future I need to come to you.'

Hasan was getting irritated by now. He raised a hand to stop him and said, 'Cut this lecture and come straight to the point, what exactly do you want from Bhai?'

Naseem smiled sheepishly and paused for a while before he spoke, he said, 'I want a chance to give Bhai a shave.'

The tension on the face of Hasan became pronounced. 'What did you say?' He said in rage, 'Did I hear you correctly? You want to...what?'

Naseem smiled and repeated his request.

Hasan angrily advanced towards Naseem, 'Is this a joke, you bastard? You have come all the way here for hajamat?'

The Don stopped him with a gesture of his hand, and then he spoke, his voice was like his appearance---normal and indistinct, 'Hasan, stop. I am sorry I have forgotten your name kid? Who did you say you were?'

'Naseem Kidwai, sir. From Jaunpur.'

'Jaunpur, near Banaras? I like Bhaiyya log. Some of my most loyal soldiers are bhaiyyas. Now tell me truly my friend Naseem, why do you want to shave me?'

Naseem took a deep breath and spoke, 'Sir a painter paints, a writer would write a story, a poet can write a poem, a photographer would take a photograph. I am a barber, and I shave. All these people will be immortalized along with you if they painted you, wrote about you or photographed you. I can see in your destiny that today you rule this city and tomorrow you will rule this world. I want to be able to tell my grand children that I had once shaved the great Shakir Ilyas.'

'That is if you HAVE grand children!' Hasan raged again. 'You stand here drivelling like a joker!'

But the Don smiled, he caught Hasan's wrist and pulled him back, 'Murtu please. I don't believe this kid is joking, nor do I think that he means any harm. These bhaiiya log are simple people with simple needs. If he wants to have something to tell his descendants then what's the harm?'

Hasan seethed but remained in his place. Naseem ignored his eyes and quietly kept his barber kit on the table in front of him. He said, 'Sir should I take that as an assent?'

The Don laughed a full laugh, and said, 'I don't see why not. You have been a good barber to Hasan. Perhaps one shave would not hurt.' The Don then looked around, 'But, where would you do it?'

Naseem slowly opened his kit and said, 'Sir even this room is good enough. I am efficient enough to make sure nothing will spill on your expensive carpet. And there is a big mirror on your side-wall. Besides you can have the shave in the comfort of your chair.'

He spread out a clean cloth on the table and spread out his instruments on it. He took out another clean towel and asked the Don if he could start the shave. Hasan stood bewildered at the corner of the room as Naseem covered the Don with the shaving cloth and started applying foam to the Don.

This was where Naseem displayed his creativity, he had bought menthol crystals and he had mixed them in the shaving cream that he had brought. It took him around 15 minutes to shave Shakir and once he had done so and applied a menthol-based aftershave lotion the don was visibly pleased.

'Not bad.' He said as he rubbed his fingers across his face. 'Hasan your barber shaves well.'

206

'Yes Bhai,' Hasan gave a disgruntled reply. 'That is why I have persisted with him; if he was bad I would have blown his head off.'

Shakir laughed and said, 'You are always in the mood for needless violence Hasan. Tell me young man, how much do I owe you?'

Naseem quickly folded his hands and said that on the contrary it was an honour to shave Shakir Ilyas and it would be sin which would send him straight to Dojakh if he accepted any money from him. Shakir was impressed with the obvious flattery and gave him a fifty rupee note to display his magnanimity. Hasan told him to accept the note in the interest of his good health.

When Hasan and Naseem walked out of the office, he brusquely told the barber to get in the car. Then he drove like a mad man to a secluded spot, asked Naseem to get out and pointed a gun on his forehead.

'Who do you think you are?'

'Sir? What happened sir...'

Hasan slapped him across the face with his other hand and said, 'Answer me! Who the hell do you think you are?'

'No one sir...no one at all...'

He was greeted with another slap. 'If you start acting over smart again you dense idiot then I am going to gift you a bullet to your head. I will not hesitate to kill you.' And to prove his intent he fired a shot near his legs.

Hasan left Naseem there and went away alone in his car. Naseem made his way to a bus stop and took a bus back to Dadar and from there took a train back to Byculla. Despite the physical violence that he had been subjected to, he was pretty happy with the outcome of the day.

The next day when he went back to the shop he expected Hasan to have created some trouble with Pasha Bhai, but his day went off normally. He was prepared for the worst, but as the day went on it occurred to him that Hasan would feel very stupid with himself if he made such a big issue of the fact that a barber had shaved his boss. That night he told an awestruck Bilal about his adventure in Bandra, for good or bad---Shakir Ilyas was a celebrity. Naseem also told him to be ready to move out and hide at a moment's notice, but he did not deem to tell him why so. Naseem told him that he will make sure that money will not be a problem.

Hasan stopped calling him over to his house for personal barber sessions, this was both a good and a bad thing for Naseem. He was happy with not having to go to the Devil's house on a monthly basis, but he also needed his plan to advance to the next level. So it was with a stroke of good luck that he received Hasan's phone one fine day.

'Bastard,' Hasan said, 'Thank whatever stars are creating this good fortune for you. Even though I do not want anything to do with you, Shakir Bhai has told me to send you over to his office one more time. Bastard you go there yourself; I am not going to drop you like I am your driver. And I hope you give Bhai a good shave otherwise I will slit your throat with your own *ustara*.'

Naseem was good with places and directions; it did not take him a long time to find out the house on Carter Road once he reached Bandra. The two guards outside the building were both the same as those present two months before. They recognized him and let him in after having a cursory glance over his barber kit.

There was a different young woman inside today, and this one was sitting on the Don's lap when Naseem knocked and entered his office. He apologized and was about to back off when the Don told him to not mind the woman and told him to prepare for his shave. To impress the Don Naseem had used even more creativity, this time he had mixed a few choice herbs in the cream after consultation with Pasha Bhai, and he had thus ensured a delightful aroma of the shaving cream. The young woman got away from the Don and observed him getting shaved. For obvious reasons she did not call Shakir bhai and instead used the word 'Sahib'. She talked incessantly while the Don got his beard shaved and moustache trimmed, talking to him about how a producer was harassing her or how she was not getting good roles. This time after the shave Naseem offered a head massage after the shave. There was a barber in Pasha Bhai's salon who had learnt the art of massaging from a famous *Pehelwan*, and Naseem had been taught by that barber. Shakir did not mind, and after the massage this time gave him a note of hundred.

That day after returning home Naseem gave the note to Bilal and told him to keep it safe, the time for spending it would come later.

Naseem noted in his diary – *Allah has been good to me by granting me unforeseeable luck thus far. I pray to Allah to give me one last chance to finish this chapter.*

There was no guarantee that Shakir Ilyas would call him for a third time. And it was highly doubtful that Hasan would contact him ever again. There was nothing else to do but to wait. In the meantime he tried to shadow Hasan and found out that he had again gone to Dubai for a few months. He also tried to spy on the Don himself but could not really discern a pattern.

It was the toughest four months that Naseem had spent in Bombay. It was a time in which he saw his plan almost coming to fruition and also never so because he had no way of contacting the Don himself and his only connection with the Don had started avoiding him completely. And with each newspaper headline he realized how important it was for his plan to complete. To cement his plan he bought a few disguises from a shop in Abdul Rahman Street and did a recce of the house in Carter Road. He also kept a regular watch at Hasan's fourth floor house in Byculla. Twice using the same disguises he went up all the way to the fourth floor to check if Hasan had returned or not. Because of his frequent visits he was already well aware of the layout of the house.

All he needed was luck.

And luck came to him on the date of 14th of August. He had got to know that Hasan had come back from Dubai around the first of the month, and even though he did not contact him or come to Pasha Bhai's shop he had once enquired whether Naseem still worked there. Pasha had asked whether he wanted the boy to be removed from the shop. Hasan had sighed and said 'Not yet.'

On the morning of 14th of August he received the call that he wanted. Hasan asked him to come on the phone and quite rudely told him to go and meet the Don. Pasha Bhai did not know that Naseed had been to Shakir Ilyas twice in the past year or so, he thought he was still shaving Hasan. Thus, when Naseem asked to borrow a clean and slightly expensive hair cut apron he did not suspect anything to be amiss.

The first thing he did was to tell Bilal to take the day off immediately, go home, pack and wait for further instructions. The second thing he did was to pack the hair cut apron and his barber kit and head towards Hasan's house.

He knocked hard on Hasan's door, not responding to the shouts of 'Who is it?' from inside. It was eleven thirty in the morning but when Hasan opened the door it seemed that he was already drunk. He had bloodshot eyes and they became completely red when he saw his guest, 'You Bastard!' he half shouted but he was stopped by a swift punch to the face. He did not expect the meek Naseem to attack him. He also did not expect the punch to be followed by a kick to the chest.

Naseem entered the house quickly and closed the door behind him. He did not allow Hasan to recover, his inebriated state helped. Hasan was lying on the floor panting because of having the wind knocked out of him. Naseem quickly opened his kit and brought out a dirty cleaning cloth from inside. He clutched Hasan's neck and forced him to open his mouth. He immediately stuffed the cleaning cloth inside, punched him again straight on the mouth and then pulled his flailing body up.

Hasan was still in a state of shock, till today he had never really sized up this taller than six feet kid who had till now been very docile. His hand quickly went to remove the cloth from his mouth but this left his stomach unprotected which left him vulnerable for another punch. Hasan fought back and landed a punch on Naseem's face, which lead to further enraging an already berserk barber. He pushed him against a wall and with a brawny fore hand held him by the neck.

'You slapped me twice that day. Do you remember?' And then he used the flat of a giant palm to slap Hasan. He got kneed in the stomach as Hasan fought to regain control; he was also able to kick Naseem's legs from under him making him fall. And then he started scrambling for the drawer next to his bed. Naseem smiled and took the risk of letting Hasan take out the gun. In the small claustrophobic house it did not take him long to hoist himself, grab Hasan's head and bash it against the wall. Hasan's grasp on the gun loosened. He grappled with Hasan and kicked his hands, not allowing him to aim or fire.

And then he took control of the gun. He held the gun and used the butt to hit the jaw of the gangster. Then he attained the brutality of a butcher and hit him repeatedly with the butt of the gun until he was almost unconscious. When he was satisfied that Hasan could not get up again he took out the barber apron from under his shirt and tied it across his neck. He lifted Hasan and propped him against a chair and then sat on top of his legs. He put the gun on his forehead and then removed the safety as he had seen Hasan do on occasion.

'I have never fired a gun before.' He said, 'and I need to make sure that I do not miss.' He roughly shoved the gun inside the mouth and said, 'Don't worry about the neighbours. If they hear a shot they will think that you are practicing shooting on birds. Remember? This is what you told me.'

And then Naseem closed his eyes and pulled the trigger. He heard two distinct sounds. first a loud report of the gun firing and then immediately after that the dull crunch of bones breaking. Naseem kept his eyes closed for a few seconds. When he opened it he saw blood, bone and viscera on his apron and a big red stain which was increasing in size on the bed sheet. It was after a little while that he realized that his hands were shaking terribly. With jittery fingers he removed his apron, wiped the gun, wiped his hands with it and removed all traces of blood from his person.

He had suspected that Hasan's comment on the neighbours not bothering with the gun shot was not a bluff. This entire neighbourhood was quite rough and a gun shot at noon would not really be out of place. To calm his nerves he helped himself to a cigarette from a tin lying on Hasan's table and with shaky hands he lit it. He smoked one sitting in one place, and then he lit another from the dying butt of the first one and started ransacking the two-room house. The first thing he did was to unplug the landline phone, and then he checked the almirah, the two bedside drawers and under the mattress. In two places he hit pay dirt, there were plastic wrappers full of notes of the same denomination---hundred. He sat down in a place and counted the money, it was around ten thousand rupees.

Naseem divided the stack of money in two equal parts, keeping one inside his barber kit and the other inside his sling bag. He went back to his own house, told Bilal that the time has come to make his escape. He gave his friend the bag along with instructions about going to hide in the city of Bhopal. The key thing, he told Bilal, was to not wait for him, and in the worst case scenario assume that Naseem is never going to come.

He left a shocked and bewildered Bilal behind him, hoping that he would act according to plan and not get cold feet at the last moment.

This was the first murder that he had ever committed, not that he had thought it would ever come to him murdering anyone. On the ramshackle red coloured bus that was taking him from Dadar to Bandra, he took out his diary and wrote as carefully as he could – *Allah please forgive me*.

When he reached the house he was disappointed to see that one of the guards was new. Fortunately the other guard recognized him and let him in. 'Bhai's barber.' He said and motioned Naseem to enter the house. The guard inside the house was the same old, so he let Naseem knock on the door twice and then told him to enter.

Naseem was greeted with a scene quite similar to the one he had seen last time, only this time it was a famous actress whom he had seen in a couple of movies who was lying on the Don's table in a state of undress and she was playfully pulling Shakir's tie. Like last time, Shakir did not consider any of this inappropriate behaviour in front of an outsider. All he did was tell her to get away from the table and sit on a chair.

'You are late.' He said, 'It is good that I had such a nice company to keep otherwise I might have become angry. This lady,' he pointed out to the actress, 'is the reason that you are here. The last time when you shaved me, I don't know what you put in the cream of yours, but this lady liked it a bit too much. I scoured many markets of Bombay, Dilli and Dubai for that scent but I could not get it. Then of course that stupid Hasan went to Dubai...never mind all that, today is a special occasion. I am in a good mood, and to celebrate I want this lady also to be in a good mood. Do you understand?'

Naseem nodded and deftly started unpacking his kit on the table. He said in a low voice, 'If Bhai does not mind, may I put forward a small request?'

The Don was already facing towards the mirror, he said, 'What is it?'

'Sir...us barber folk, we...we are not used to working in front of a *zanana* eye. Our parlours are men's only.'

'This is not your parlour,' the Don said, 'This is my office.'

'I agree sir, it is just that...if only for fifteen minutes if the Bibi ji can excuse us then...I might feel a bit more comfortable sir.'

The Don looked slightly annoyed, he looked at his watch and said, 'Ok ! I am giving you not just fifteen minutes but half an hour. After that she comes back inside the office, whether you have finished or not.' He turned towards the actress and said, 'Mani, could you please wait outside for half an hour? Or better still, why not take the car and Javed and get me some of those sweet rolls from that bakery in front of Mehboob Studio.'

'Jaanu do I have to go? Are those rolls sweeter than me?'

The Don laughed and said, 'Of course nothing is sweeter than you. But come on, be a sport and get me some, won't you?' And then he dismissed her with a motion of the hand. The film actress stomped her foot in mock anger and went out of the room. Naseem checked his own wrist watch, knowing well that he had only half an hour to complete his task.

He took his time in applying lather on the Don's face, letting him get a proper whiff of the scent that he wanted. While applying the cream he kept on talking to the Don, 'Sir, I am really grateful to you for giving me this chance once again. I always keep on feeling that every time that I get to serve you might be the last time.' The Don gave a non-committal grunt in reply.

'Sir over the course of your business,' Naseem continued, 'you must have come across many tough situations. You must have literally played with danger. Is it true?' Shakir gave an imperceptible nod.

'Sir, is it really like it is shown in the films? Like that car chase in Don? Have you really escaped from a hail of bullets?'

The don smiled indulgently at his filmy fan and nodded. Naseem acted pleased, 'I knew it sir. I know you are no less than Amitabh Bachchan.'

After applying the lather Naseem started clearing it up, 'Sir have you ever had a one on one gun fight with anyone?'

The don nodded in the affirmative. Then he stole a quick glance at the watch.

'Sir, has anyone held you at gun point? A gun sticking to your head?'

The don shook his head slightly, saying no. He appeared irritated by this particular question.

'Sir, has anyone held a knife to your throat?'

The Don again dismissed his question with a quick no and then brought his wrist up to properly look at the time.

'Sir, do you know you have allowed me to put a sharpened knife to your throat?'

And before the Don could realize that Naseem had replaced his Ustara with a sharp switch-blade, the barber had already applied almost superhuman speed and force and cut off his jugular. A spurt of blood shot out from his neck as the Don screamed (but to no avail since they were inside a specially constructed soundproof room). Naseem plunged the knife in the side of Shakir's neck and then immediately brought out his ustara to widen the first cut. Shakir was losing blood and energy rapidly, he tried to get up to fight but couldn't because Naseem had tied the long towel in a double knot around his neck and the chair. As the Don grappled with the edge of the towel Naseem quickly moved to the front of him and repeatedly stabbed his stomach using the blade.

In a last bid attempt to save his life Shakir toppled his chair and fell down, trying to move from under the towel. Naseem stomped his size ten foot on the base of his neck, making more blood spurt out. He jumped on the Don's chest twice, and then kicked violently at his head, trying to sever it away from the neck. The man on the floor tried in vain to stop the flow of kicks using his hands as a shield, and once or twice managed to do so, but by the time he had lost a lot of blood and was thus losing whatever energy that he had. Naseem stopped kicking him and bent down, keeping one knee on the criminal's chest he started at the neck again with the knife, slashing at it the way a coconut seller slices the top end of the fruit.

He counted sixty strokes on the neck before the head and the rest of the body were connected only by a few sinews, some muscle and cartilage. If the man prostrate before him was still alive then he was truly the Devil and thus deserved to live.

The next thing that he did was to remove the expensive watch from Shakir's wrist. He had a look at the time when the Don had asked the girl to go. From then till now around twenty minutes had elapsed. It had taken him ten minutes to kill the gangster. In the adrenaline rush that followed he was pleased to note that The Most Wanted Man in Bombay was at the end of it all a Man. And whatever *buri aatma* resided inside him had flown away to *dozakh* through the gaping hole in his neck. He pocketed the watch, hastily cleaned his ustara and the switch blade on the towel lying on the floor. Then he removed his blood splattered kurta and wiped his hands and face with it. He was wearing another shirt beneath it; there were slight signs of blood on his inner shirt but not too pronounced to arouse suspicion. He balled up the kurta and the towel, opened the toilet attached to the room and dumped it inside the pot.

Now Naseem was in a fix. In hindsight this was the easy part---killing an unarmed man with a knife. What followed was going to very tough, he had to escape from this house which had two guards stationed outside the main gate and the third guard and that young woman were due back within a few minutes. He also had no way of knowing whether they had already returned and were waiting without, the woman eager to come in once the thirty minutes pass.

He was sure that all three of the guards would be carrying handguns, and he knew that his set of knives wasn't going to do well in a gun fight. He would not be able to force his way out of this house by fighting the guards. There was only one thing that he could do now---find a way to escape.

He mentally mapped the house in his head, this room that he was in was directly in front of the main door. Although this room was windowless, he knew there was a ventilator in the toilet which faced exactly opposite the main gate. He quickly closed the door to this room from the inside to buy more time and then he used all his strength to push the table in the room against the door. Then he went inside the toilet with his kit and locked it from inside too.

He did not know when the guards will realize that something is amiss, he also had no idea how long will it take for them to come inside once they start attacking the door. He checked the wrist watch to realize that there were only a couple of minutes for the half an hour to get over. He looked at the ventilator. Because of the small bite-sized rooms of Bombay, the ventilator was at an optimum height for him to escape from it.

The ventilator had four slanted glass panes, and he knew he had to carefully remove each one of them to make sure that they did not break. He was sure that the room was soundproof but he knew the same could not be said with certainty about the toilet.

By the time he had removed the last panel he could hear a dull but frantic thumping on the main door of the room. He clutched his kit box tightly in one hand and hoisted himself up on the ventilator. He could see that there was a boundary wall in front of him at a space of about three feet away. He clumsily threw his kit over the wall. And then he started pushing himself out of the tight space, when he was half way out he pushed his hands against the wall in front and using the friction of the rough paint he started hoisting his torso upwards until his hands grabbed the edge of the wall. He winced in pain as he discovered the hard way that the wall was covered with small shards of glass. He tried to ignore the pain and the cuts on his hand and brought his knees up to rest on the ledge of the ventilator. Now he was almost parallel to the ground.

At that exact moment he heard a loud thumping from the bathroom door along with hysterical shouting from the Don's room. He held on tightly to the top of the wall, took a deep breath and with Allah's name on his lips he coiled his body and sprang away from the ventilator and over the top of the wall.

He had miscalculated his jump and his feet hit the wall on his way over. He landed with a loud thud on his left shoulder, and in that moment of pain and confusion he was quite sure that he had heard a bullet being fired behind him.

He was in a narrow lane with houses lined on both sides, and with the sense of self-preservation that was still left in him he picked up his barber kit and started to run. He ran like a mad man in the labyrinthine lanes of the Christian part of Bandra West, he remembered knocking over at least two people in his mad dash to get to safety. About two kilometres away from Shakir's place he came across the main road, he slowed his pace and caught the first bus that was speeding away.

When the conductor asked him for his destination he said absent minded 'the last stop.' And then he started laughing wildly. He laughed as relief spread across him. He laughed because a barber had done what few men could even dream of doing. He laughed because he had fulfilled a promise he made to himself and delivered not one but two devils to hell. And in the end he laughed because he was still alive, and being alive had never felt this good before.

The bus that day took him to Borivali from where he caught a train to Ahmedabad, and after buying new clothes in the city and spending a day there he travelled in general compartment in Sabarmati Express to reach Bhopal, staying awake for the duration of the journey.

For five years Naseem and Bilal changed cities, working as apprentice barbers or as sales men in shops. For two years they lived in the constant fear and thrill of being targeted and killed by the Bombay mafia. Naseem tried to ignore the fact that there would have been reprisals against Pasha Bhai's barbershop. He reasoned that Pasha Bhai had a lot of underworld contacts that would protect him.

It was a difficult thing for the Bombay underworld to digest that Shakir Ilyas had been outwitted and killed by a barber. They used their sources in the police and the media to suppress this news, choosing instead to report that he had died abroad due to a health complication. This young barber had become a mythic figure, but because his only major link to the Don was Hasan Murtuza, who in turn was linked only to Pasha Bhai, and because no one really bothers to know the background or family history of a barber, the massive manhunt to catch Naseem was limited only to the city of Bombay. At the end of five years the Underworld gave up on most of its efforts, keeping this particular vengeance pending.

Naseem continued fighting crime, initially on a small scale, using his knives in dispatching criminals in small cities of MP like Katni, Satna and Meher. While Bilal did not follow suit in his vigilantism, he helped Naseem carefully spend the money that they had stolen from Hasan Murtuza. They saved most of the money they earned, living frugally. They finally settled in Indore, where they had a chance of earning more. Here Bilal decided to stay for a long time, and thus started his family. Naseem stayed single, vowing to do the best he could.

And then at the end of ten years of his self-imposed exile, he returned to Mumbai. The money that he had taken from the city had multiplied many times, and even after splitting it half with Bilal he was left with a decent amount to start his life afresh. He was no longer the young boy who had come here with a small steel attaché. Naseem had filled out and looked impressive with long hair and an equally long beard.

He took a small shop for rent in Colaba, and started giving employment to youth from Azamgarh, Jaunpur and Banaras. Out of his employees, every year he would select one worker who seemed similar to the young Naseem who had managed to achieve the impossible. And then he would train him in the cause of his own holy war, and the need to slowly erode the scum of the underworld from his adopted home.

Presently Mr Naseem Kidwai sat outside his shop, smoking a cigarette contentedly in the rain. There had been eleven gangster deaths, both major and minor which he and his barber syndicate had caused. He was looking forward to writing another page of his life in his notebook which he kept carefully along with other souvenirs of life of crime fighting, including an expensive watch soaked in blood. He treated the fifteenth of August as the beginning of a new year, and he regarded a new boy who had joined his shop keenly. He saw in his eyes the same slow fire that had burnt continuously within him for the past quarter of a century. Fifteenth was going to be an auspicious day for that boy's induction.

Naseem got up and doused the cigarette with a few rain drops. He smiled as he walked back inside his shop. He had to train another recruit; the Barber's war needed more soldiers.